What people are saying about

So Very

There's a warmth in C.C. Howard's debut that wraps itself around you like the best of Hornby or Doyle. Music, football, love and kindness – I was hooked.
Richard Jobson, singer-songwriter for Skids, filmmaker, TV presenter and author of *Into the Valley*

A fun, fast-paced, geeky romp. C.C. Howard's debut is as engaging as it is challenging. I loved it!
Melanie Cantor, author of *Death and Other Happy Endings*

So Very Mental

So Very Mental

C.C. Howard

Winchester, UK
Washington, USA

JOHN HUNT PUBLISHING

First published by Roundfire Books, 2022
Roundfire Books is an imprint of John Hunt Publishing Ltd., No. 3 East St., Alresford, Hampshire SO24 9EE, UK
office@jhpbooks.com
www.johnhuntpublishing.com
www.roundfire-books.com

For distributor details and how to order please visit the 'Ordering' section on our website.

ISBN: 978 1 78904 919 0
978 1 78904 920 6 (ebook)
Library of Congress Control Number: 2021942217

A CIP catalogue record for this book is available from the British Library.

Design: Stuart Davies

UK: Printed and bound by CPI Group (UK) Ltd, Croydon, CR0 4YY
Printed in North America by CPI GPS partners

For my beautiful & brilliant daughter Beatrice

Part One

1

She sat me down and patted my hand. 'Your problem Howie,' she said, 'is that you have no interests.' This marked the beginning of the end for me and Carrie O'Donnell.

Carrie was twenty-eight at the time and smart and beautiful. I don't know if her beauty was conventional or apparent to everyone, but I couldn't escape my attraction to her: the way she twirled her hair, the impossibly fine hair on her arms, the unbuttoned jeans that fit her buttocks perfectly. I could just stare at her all day. She used to watch TV with her head tilted sideways and I used to watch her watching TV. She would turn her head towards me questioningly, contemptuously really, and I would say something stupid like: 'You're going to do damage to your neck if you keep watching TV that way.' She would likely tell me, in a quiet, disconcerting voice, to 'fuck off' and then she would tilt her head again and continue watching. And I would just keep on watching her. Of course, if there was a game on, I wouldn't be watching her at all. I'd be watching the game. But then, Carrie wouldn't be sat watching the football anyway. Carrie wasn't interested in football and couldn't understand why anyone would be. And that's what I'm getting at, really. Carrie said I wasn't interested in anything, but the truth was, I just wasn't interested in anything she was interested in.

For instance, Carrie was very interested in design. It wasn't any specific form or type; she was interested in the design of all 'things'. She'd pick up an object, any object, and say, 'This is well designed.'

'It's a cardboard box,' I'd say.

'It's well designed though, isn't it?'

And, over the years, it would go on like that:

'It's a chair!'

'It's a magazine!'

'It's a kettle!'

'Yeah, but it's well designed though, isn't it?'

We would argue about these kinds of things. These arguments were usually along the lines of design versus functionality. I mean, to state my case, what is the point of something if it doesn't work? Am I right? And if it works, why does it need to look good? Our arguments were often ended with Carrie sighing and looking at me as if I was some kind of small wild animal that, for its own sake, needed to be ushered back into the woods. And then she would finish me by telling me I have no interests.

'Fuck off, Carrie,' I would mumble under my breath.

I never won an argument. In all those six or so years. She would always walk away smiling.

I was rather pathetic, when I think about it. I don't know if much has changed.

But what did Carrie know anyway? I have interests. Pff! Of course I have interests. Sure, you can count them on one hand, in fact with just three fingers, but I have them. And I happen to know that my interests are shared by other people – like-minded people and interesting people. Not everyone is into design, *Carrie*!

Anyway, as I've been banging on about my interests so much, it seems silly not to lay them out, get them down in black and white, so to speak. Here they are, in no particular order:

1: Space (as in 'outer'.)

2: Music (*Good* music. Don't get me started.)

3: The Arsenal (as in the football club.)

I'm aware they look a bit silly placed in a list like this. There's much more to my life than these three interests, I can assure you, but I will come to those other things later. For now, I'd like to explain myself. For the benefit of Carrie, and anyone else out there whose interests are more, let's say, high brow, I'd like to explain why I love these things and why, if I didn't have them, well, what the fuck *would* I have exactly?

Firstly, space. *Space!* I mean who isn't interested in space? Carrie? Carrie would probably say it wasn't well designed. And who knows? Maybe she'd be right. But that's a philosophical argument I'm not prepared to have right now…(*Carrie*!)

Space! If you ever care to look up into the sky on a cloudless night, how could you not be overwhelmed by the mystic beauty, the terrifying immensity and the baffling questions it poses about human existence? Well, to be honest, I don't allow myself to wallow too much on the latter of these ponderings. Life is too short. And besides, if you allow yourself to feel the awe of *what* is, do you really need to know *why* it is?

I can still hear Carl Sagan muttering 'billions and billions' or 'millions, billions and trillions' on his TV show of the eighties, *Cosmos*. I saw it as a young lad, on a rerun, and I was transfixed for life. Now I consume any and all TV shows about space. Naturally, I've marvelled at the pictures of Uranus and Neptune sent back by Voyager 2, the images of galaxies and nebulas given to us by the Hubble Telescope and, of course, there are the rovers on Mars. And all the fascinating stories: the astronauts, the dramatic launches, the near misses, the tragedies, the heroic escapes and the moon landings. The endless chatter about incomprehensible physics, all the black-hole speculation and bizarre theories, the crazy knowledge of the observable unseeable. It's endlessly fascinating, isn't it? *Billions and billions* of suns, of solar systems, of galaxies and trillions of planets. How can one not marvel at the scope of it all? How can one not look up and marvel? Of course, if you live in London, as I do, what you usually see when you look up is a blanket of clouds, blindingly reflecting the glow of a city's electric light. But anyway, you surely know what I mean. It's the very thought of it all. It's a wonder. It's beyond a wonder.

Chapstick, my best mate, he gets overwhelmed when I throw the numbers at him. He gets anxiety, a pain in his gut, and he insists I stop. But I can't help it:

'13.8 billion light years,' I tell him.

'What? No...'

'At least that's what is observable.'

'Observable?'

'Think about it. That light from the edge of our universe has taken 13.8 billion years to get to us, so in that time, the universe has been expanding even further. Rough estimates say that, at this minute, the universe is probably about 90 billion light years in diameter. Amazing, yeah?'

'You're doing my head in. Isn't it your round?'

'And you know the Milky Way?'

'The chocolate bar?'

'It's a galaxy, right? And they estimate that most galaxies contain around 100 billion stars.'

'This is *literally* hurting my head.'

'And say there are a trillion galaxies, and they estimate...'

'I'll get my own beer. If you're still talking about space when I get back, I'm going home.'

I'm not going to go into everything I know about space. I'm not like Carrie. I don't assume that everyone is interested in what I am interested in. Suffice to say, I could hurt Chapstick's brain a lot more, but I'm not inclined to. He's my mate, and, luckily, he shares my other interests. And anyway, just to be clear, I'm not pretending here that I know everything about space. That's not the point. Compared to the scientists, physicists and astronomers, I know practically nothing. But that's not what I'm getting at. Space, and its endless wonder, will never fail to rouse my curiosity. I can't get enough of it. And surely that constitutes an interest, right? And what I am saying is, well, if you haven't figured it out, Carrie was well wrong about me.

Interests. Pff. I've got interests! I've got three of them! Three!

So let me come on to the easy one: music. Who doesn't like music? Truthfully, I think everyone has a special place for music in their lives, don't they? But there are those that like it, I guess, and then there are those that can't live without it. I am not giving out prizes to those that can guess which category I belong to. Suffice to say, I live and breathe it. When the Beach Boys sing 'God Only Knows', the greatest pop song ever, I think they are singing about music itself. It's meta, right? (That song, by the way, is about as close to perfect as pop will ever get. *Fact.*)

Chapstick and I spend a lot of time in music shops, looking for old vinyl records. You know what they say: you've got to listen to it on vinyl; everything else is pretty much obsolete. CDs, Mp3s and the rest, just not good enough, sonically speaking. But of course you can't get everything on vinyl these days. We do lapse into digital every now and then, but, as Chapstick says, 'If it isn't on vinyl, or wasn't at some point or other, it's probably not worth listening to anyway.' We call ourselves purists. Carrie used to call me a music snob. If she'd only listened to herself saying that, then perhaps she would never have said that I have no interests. I mean, how could I be a music snob if I wasn't interested in music? Am I right?

'You don't *listen* to music,' she once told me. 'You *pretend* to listen to music.'

'What do you mean?' I snapped back, gobsmacked.

'I mean,' she said calmly, 'it's an intellectual pursuit for you, not emotional. Music is supposed to be about emotions.'

'You do realize there was a band called The Emotions? Just saying. From Chicago. Started out as gospel and ended up cashing in on disco in the seventies. You can dance to them. I think you'd like them.'

She sighed audibly and shook her head and walked away. She'd won another argument, without even having to close. She could do that. She could win arguments by breathing in a certain way, or smiling. She even winked at me once, but she never did that again because I winked back, multiple times, as if I had a tic. For fuck's sake, nothing worked. Nothing I did would ever work with her.

I guess by now it's becoming obvious why Carrie and I didn't work out. But let me come back to her later. That voice in my head, that voice I deride as *Carrie*, is getting a little too much airplay right now.

More importantly, and now that I've slipped into my passion for music, I should lend a few lines to my best bud, Chapstick. I've already mentioned him, of course, but his importance in my life cannot be overstated. And it's fair to say that music has played a big part in our lives. Without it, Chapstick and I might not be friends at all, let alone best friends. And who knows, without Chapstick, maybe, just maybe, music wouldn't mean so much to me.

So, as said, Chapstick is my best buddy. No doubt about it. We went to school together, through all the levels, we played football (badly) together, but I think it's fair to say that it was our mutual, burgeoning interest in music that really bonded us. Oh, and the Arsenal, of course, but I haven't got to the Gunners yet.

Chapstick is East Asian, Chinese I think, or at least his parents are. He was born in England in fact, but he has, you know, slanty eyes, black hair and he's kind of small. I don't know if I just described the stereotypical Asian just now, and I don't mean anything by it. It's not that he looks like all other Chinese or anything. And I'm not saying all other Chinese look the same as each other either, just for the record. I'm just saying, you know, he has slanty eyes and black hair. Fact.

His real name is Eddie Song, just about the coolest fucking name anyone could ever have, really. But in primary school, and high school, everyone called him Chopstick. I did too, and I didn't think much of it till my first girlfriend, Anna, said I was being racist. *Racist?* What the fuck?

'I love Chopstick, you dickwad!'

1

'You're well racist, calling him that!'

'Fuck off! I love him. I love his little slanty eyes and the fact that he's bumless.'

'Hey,' said Chapstick, listening in. 'I've got a bum!'

'It's well racist,' Anna insisted.

Both Chapstick and I just shrugged.

But I gave it all some thought, you know. I mean, it's not as though he looked like a chopstick, or if he even knew how to use one. The guy was retarded even with a knife and fork. But it did make me think. In fact, Anna had a way of making me think. She was always putting things to me. You can't say this. You can't do that. You shouldn't put that there. Etc. When I come to think of it, Anna was right bossy. I was her pussy-boy. That about sums it up. Pathetic. Oh, but let me come back to Anna later.

I started calling Chopstick Chapstick. I told him it made sense. He had very soft sensual lips. 'You even use a ChapStick, don't you?'

'Yeah, but why don't you just call me by my name?'

'Nah, wouldn't be right, would it? You have to have a nickname.'

He shrugged, and ever since then he's been called Chapstick.

It's an understatement to say that Chapstick and I bond over music. Our weekly routines are all bent around music. (Well, Saturdays are for football, but I am coming to that.) We scour record shops on Monday and Wednesday evenings and on Fridays, after a few beers at the pub, we go home to either his place or mine and play records. We only have a few rules:

1: Bob Dylan and Miles Davis are the supreme-leader-geniuses of the last one hundred years of music (the Picassos of the music world). No one else comes close. No arguments. Full stop. Fact.

2: A country song is only really a country song if you can imagine George Jones and/or Tammy Wynette singing it. Fact.

3: Digital players are allowed for listening on one condition: that there is evidence that the vinyl record of said artist exists, but is currently impossible to obtain. (We have a shared Spotify account for such undesirable occurrences.)

Oh and then there's this rule:

4: When my brother, Ben, who has autism, is around, *Bitches Brew* is not to be played.

And just to emphasize, this last rule is important. Whenever that record is put on and Ben is around, he gets very upset, puts his hands over his ears and cries: 'Make it stop, Howie! Make it stop!' Thankfully he doesn't hate all Miles Davis. When I put on the song 'It Never Entered My Mind' he nods and says, 'I like this one, Howie. I really like this one!' We smile at each other, feeling the safe place in the music.

I can't put into words how much I love my brother, Ben. But much more about Ben very soon.

Chapstick and I disagree about very little when it comes to music. At a stretch, his favourite Miles album is *Sketches of Spain*, and mine is *In a Silent Way*. His favourite Dylan is *Blood on the Tracks*. Mine is *Blonde on Blonde*. But for the most part, we're on the same page.

Just last week Chapstick came over with a Van Morrison album and played the track 'When Heart Is Open'. He said, whispering, using that music-discovery voice he has: 'You hear that? It sounds like *In a Silent Way*.'

'Holy fuck!' I said. 'It *does* sound like *In a Silent Way*.'

We love moments like that. We barely have to speak. We just look at each other, excited as fuck.

'He must have been listening to Miles at the time,' Chapstick mumbled, as he fumbled with the needle, looking to play the intro over.

'Well, Van always did talk about jazz. His dad was a jazz man, I think. It's troubling to hear this, bro. Why haven't we noticed this before?'

'We can't listen to everything.'

'I guess.'

'It's pretty cool though.'

'Yeah, let's listen to it again.'

So, in the pub last Friday, I got about espousing a music theory I had been sitting on. We were on our third beer, and we were drinking with a guy called Pontiac. Pontiac is a guy we meet at the pub occasionally, mostly on Saturdays. He's tall. I think his parents are Jamaican, so sometimes we greet him like we are *Rastas* and he just shakes his head and calls us idiots. Pontiac likes music as much as we do, but he doesn't comply with our rules. He says he acknowledges Dylan's influence, but suggests that the baton was passed on years ago, to guys like Neil Young and James Taylor. When Chapstick and I hear such blasphemy we just look at each other. We don't even need to roll our eyes. For us, anyone who says they are into music, and they don't listen to Dylan, well, they are missing the whole point of everything. As for Miles, Pontiac says that he owns just one of his records.

'Let me guess,' said Chapstick, rolling his eyes contemptuously. '*Kind of Blue*.'

Pontiac nodded and we all knew that it was true. If there was one jazz album in anyone's collection, it was *Kind of Blue*. Pontiac doesn't shy away from the truth, which is what we like about him. And he has good ideas and theories himself, like the time he said:

'Every great band, and we are talking great, not good... Every great band needs two things: a great distinctive riff-master, song-writing guitarist and a great lyric-writing singer-front-man.'

'Richards and Jagger,' said Chapstick.

'Marr and Morrissey,' I said.

'Jones and Strummer,' Chapstick came back.

'Page and Plant,' I said.

Pontiac pointed at us, one at a time, as if to say, *Yeah, you get it*. We riffed on that idea for hours. It was a good theory.

But on Friday I wanted to talk to them about my latest theory, the idea of the most overrated underrated bands of all time.

'What does that mean?' asked Pontiac. 'Give me an example.'

'The Grateful Dead,' I said.

They both nodded and waited for me to explain.

'A good band. One of the truly great and innovative guitarists of all time in Jerry Garcia.'

'But no real front man,' said Pontiac.

'Yes, that's true. They lacked a decent singer, though dead-heads will argue against this till they're blue in the face. And it's true, beyond Jerry – the genius – the rest of them were just very good musicians. But let's give them credit, there's a few unforgettable live recordings.'

'I think my favourite GD album is still *Hundred Years Hall*,' said Chapstick. 'But I'm no dead-head.'

'They noodle a little too much for me,' said Pontiac. 'It's all very masturbatory.'

'The idea of the most overrated underrated bands,' I continued, 'is based on this: firstly, the band has to have a sizeable devoted fan base. In the case of the *Dead* they even have a name for a die-hard fan. And because the Grateful Dead, apart from a surprising, momentary breakout in the eighties, has remained largely under the radar, they somehow are, for the most part, ignored by the masses. My theory encapsulates the idea that a loyal fan of a largely ignored band considers his band to be underrated. And in order to try and set things right, they overcompensate, by grossly overrating the band. Hence, an overrated underrated band.'

'Interesting,' said Pontiac. 'I know this dead-head. It's like he never shuts up about the band. It's like he never listens to anything else.'

'Exactly!' I said.

'Any more examples?'

'Steely Dan maybe? Radiohead? The band has to be kinda outside the mainstream, but has to have a big fan base. Popular, but not popular in the pop-music sense.'

'What about underrated underrated bands?' asked Chapstick.

'Interesting,' I said. 'Go on.'

We could go on like that for hours. Waffling. Music is a subject that one never really tires of, if it's an interest. And that's just it: who would talk about stuff like this for hours if they weren't interested in it? And what music did Carrie like anyway? Well how should I know? She never listened to music as far as I could discern. Not *really* listen. Like, listen in the way Chapstick and I would. Anyway...

* * *

Saturdays are all about the football, or, to be more precise, all about the Arsenal. Well, sometimes it's Sundays. In fact, now that we are a Europa League team, it's mostly Sundays, which kind of sucks. We – Chapstick, Ben and I – love our Saturday afternoons, the three o'clock kick off, going down to the Emirates and yelling and singing for two hours. More often than not our team seems to lose these days, and it gets us down and makes us wonder why we are putting ourselves through it, but it's the Arsenal. It's our team. It's in our blood. And it doesn't take long till the optimism comes back. As Chapstick likes to point out: 'There's always the lower table fodder to feed on'. We'll be okay. Occasionally we'll be pretty good. It's the way it goes.

Arsenal got into my blood back in the nineties when Dennis Bergkamp signed. I shouldn't really support a North London team, seeing as I'm from South London, but I just loved Bergkamp. He was so elegant. Somehow classy. A gazelle in a world of clumsy mooses. (Or is it 'meese'?) But he could also crush bones when necessary.

Dennis Bergkamp! Dennis Bergkamp! Dennis Bergkamp! Chapstick loves to shout this every time I bring the guy's name up. It's a reference to that last minute goal he scored against Argentina in the quarter-finals of the '98 world cup. The Dutch commentator in the YouTube clip almost loses his nut. He literally does lose his voice. *Dennis Bergka...!* It's one of the great moments of tournament football.

'Not his greatest goal though,' Ben, my brother, often points out. Ben has an encyclopaedic memory of everything Arsenal.

'Newcastle 2002?' I ask him.

'That is correct, Howie. One hundred points to Howie.'

Of course Arsène Wenger joined Arsenal not long after Bergkamp's arrival and, for the next eight years or so, we were unbelievable. Unstoppable. And, during one incredible year, invincible. Those were the days, the years – the Highbury years, no less. Trophies and Wenger-ball. It was glorious. Think about it, all those players: Ian, Patrick, David, Emmanuel, Thierry, Freddie, Robert, Tony, Lee, Ray, and the 'Invisible Wall'... The list goes on and on. What a time! Years and years of unrelenting pleasure. Chapstick and I, when we aren't talking about music, we're usually talking about the glory days of the Arsenal. Of course, Ben is usually on hand too, to correct our misplaced facts and make sure our conversations are chronological and factual.

Well, everyone knows we moved from Highbury to the Emirates in 2006 and ever since we've been pretty shite. Not completely shite, as I'm sure Ben would point out, but on a slippery slope of shiteness that has culminated in our current crises. We are a club that is always in crisis now. That's just the way it is. I've been told by opposing fans that our expectations are too high and that our recent history has given us an unrealistic view on how things should be. I don't know. I just want to see my team win. Am I right?

Our Saturdays usually go like this. We meet at our station

and take the tube up to Finsbury Park and then we walk to the stadium. We started doing this way back in the day and, because of Ben, we have to do it in exactly the same way every week. Ben hates the Piccadilly line. In fact, he doesn't like the colours navy or dark blue. He hates Chelsea, of course. We tried going to Stamford Bridge once, but even though we had our very expensive away tickets, we couldn't enter the ground because Ben freaked out. We sat in Brompton Cemetery for a few hours until Ben calmed down. We lost five to one anyway, that day. An embarrassment. Ben was strangely calmed by our loss. Ever since then I've noticed that he gets quiet for a bit when we lose, but then later he looks oddly comforted. I guess he has come to expect it. And for Ben, there is nothing more comforting than expectations being fulfilled. I guess the Arsenal losing has become his new normal.

We are season ticket holders. These days we don't do away matches. It's just too hard, especially as we are playing more and more on Sundays. I've got Ben to take care of, work on Mondays, and Chapstick eventually gave up too. He felt like he was betraying himself by making digital playlists for the bus ride. It had to stop.

We're on the lower seats of the upper tier, in the corner opposite the away seats. We talk about missing Highbury all the time, but the Emirates sure is a thing of beauty. I love sitting there, cold winter days – it's so cold sometimes – and just looking around and hearing the chants, the singing, the grumbles, swearing, the booing. Sometimes I just sit there, before the lads come on, and just look around. What an immense thing. All these people. Collective optimism. A sense of good cheer and camaraderie. And then the game begins, and it's all downhill from there. Our hearts collectively begin to sink. You can almost hear the chorused sigh. We often walk out after the game saying things like: 'Oh well, there's always next week.'

The season ticket holders around us are nice, for the most

part. There's ol' Badger, who sits in front a few seats away. We call her Badger because she has a strip of white hair that flows through her otherwise very black hair. She says it just went that way, overnight. Like that stream of hair just died, or something. Anyway, she's very nice. Greets us with: 'How are the boys today then? Glass half full, is it?' She pays a lot of attention to Ben and Ben likes her. But I wish he'd stop calling her Badger to her face. That's embarrassing. Anyway, she's a real sport and she doesn't seem to mind. She's the only one in our near vicinity that doesn't spend the two hours swearing, usually at the ref. She usually says things like: 'Oh well.'

Mickie Jones sits on my right (Ben sits to my left between me and Chapstick). Mickie is a wonderful guy, until the ref blows for kick off. And then he transforms into a monster. If we're winning, he's usually okay, but if we go down, especially in the opening fifteen minutes or so, he's usually saying things like: 'That's it! We're done! We fucking ain't coming back from this!' He's a sixty-year-old man. Sometimes I worry for him. Sometimes I think he is going to have a heart attack.

Roger who sits behind us, he's well into his seventies. Or maybe he's older. I've never asked. Roger has pretty much seen it all. He goes right back to the sixties with Arsenal. And he even talks about his dad going to matches before that. He's a true Arsenal man, that's for sure. Roger usually talks about how it used to be better. How the club was a fan's club back in the day. 'They don't give a shite about us anymore. It's all about the commerciality and the money. Emirates my arse. And those billionaire owners. Don't get me started on those billionaire owners. Don't give a shite, they don't.'

It goes on and on, and he makes good points and all, but his negativity can be bad for Ben sometimes. I bought these earmuffs for Ben, for moments when things get a little too loud for him, or when he feels anxiety. When Roger goes off on one of his rants, I put the muffs on Ben and give him some hard-boiled sweets.

He says: 'Okay, Howie. It's kick off soon, Howie. I need the earmuffs. You are correct about that.'

(Did I mention that my brother, Ben, is a sweetheart? I will come back to Ben. I *have to* come back to Ben.)

What we like about the three o'clock kick off is that we can go to the pub afterwards and get a pub dinner. Ben likes his pub dinners. We have to tube-it away from the Emirates though. Some of those pubs around the stadium get too packed and they can be pretty melancholic after a defeat. And for Ben, it's even worse after we win. All the screaming and the singing, in close proximity, it all gets a little too much for him. So we usually head back to South London and go to our local, a small pub that never gets crowded and is never a fuss. And everyone knows Ben there and treats him like royalty.

Last Saturday was Ben's birthday and the locals at the pub all gave him small gifts. Things like drawing paper and pens (Ben loves to draw) and someone, Bea, gave him a new Arsenal shirt, a number 10. How fucking cool is that?

'You shouldn't have, Bea,' I said.

Bea is fifty-five. She has flowing silver hair. She probably drinks too much. But then they all do, the locals. They're all there at the bar pretty much every day. But Bea is a lovely human being. She often sits with Ben and plays chess with him. Ben is very good at chess. He usually wins and she tells him how brilliant he is.

'I have a son,' she once told me. 'He won't talk to me, or even let me see his children – my grandchildren.'

We've heard this sad story a lot. Chapstick thinks she must have done something pretty bad for her son to disown her, but I can't believe that Bea would knowingly do anything bad. I just can't see it. So, I tell Chapstick that I can't believe it, and we leave it at that.

Luckily Pontiac was there this Saturday just passed. He

usually does drop in on Fridays and Saturdays. But it was just as well this Saturday because we had just lost to our North London sworn enemies and Pontiac couldn't give one royal fuck about the North London Derby. He doesn't even like football. So we started talking music. He said he had been thinking about my theory about the most overrated underrated bands and he thought that Joy Division might qualify.

'Maybe,' I said, 'but do they have a massive fanbase? I don't know.'

Anyway, we started talking music and it took our minds off the loss. Ben ate his food – pie and mash – in peace and afterwards was happy to play cards with Bea and her boyfriend, Topper.

Topper, by the way, is another occasional source of conversation for me and Chapstick. He is our age. He is slim, good looking and works out at the gym. He also has a kind of charm, you know, that women usually like. But for some reason he is dating this woman almost twenty years his senior. Don't get me wrong. I like Bea and all, I really do, but she's not, well, sexy, for want of a better term. I don't know. To each their own, I suppose.

And that is our typical Saturday.

So as you can see, if there was any argument about me having interests before, there shouldn't be now. It's obvious that Carrie was wrong. In so many ways, Carrie was wrong. And I'm not finished with Carrie yet. Well, technically, yes, we are finished as a couple. But I am not finished talking about her, or Anna, or Bridget (my most recent ex-girlfriend). Everything I do in this story is informed by them, by their influence, and by the sheer fucked-uppery of my head when it comes to the opposite sex. But that's for soon.

Next, I want to talk about my brother, Ben, some more. It's impossible to say how important my brother is to me. It's impossible to take him out of my life and expect that I would still be, somehow, me, Howie. Yes, no, I wouldn't be Howie without Ben. Perhaps I wouldn't be at all.

2

Today I had to take Ben to the Mental Health Centre. We used to go weekly, but now we only go once a month. That is partly because I have taken on the role of his caregiver and partly because, once he turned thirty, they claimed there was little they could do with him within the public system. The monthly visits are simply check-ups. He's thirty-five now. And he's doing okay. He has me. When Mum died, a few years ago, it was up to me. I knew it would be up to me one day. I always knew I would end up taking care of Ben. It's not something I've chosen; it's something that's chosen me.

I don't really have much energy to go on about my parents, but I can take a very quick stab. Our father was an alcoholic, who left us when I was nine and Ben was six. I can't tell you if he is still alive. I know that sounds outrageous and improbable, but I've never looked him up. He was a terror to Ben when Ben was little. He just didn't get the kid. And Ben wouldn't speak and when Ben wouldn't speak, Dad used to smack him. Yes, my father was an arsehole. He never paid child support. He never looked us up. He just disappeared when things weren't going his way. So why would I look him up?

Okay. Okay. I did look him up online one day. It was a while ago. Perhaps ten years ago. He was living in Glasgow apparently. He had a whole other family up there from what I could see. I never told Mum I tracked him down. And I never told Ben. I just let it be. What good would it do to reach out to such a man? And besides, Ben remembers. And that's the thing about people with autism. People think they are stupid, but they aren't at all. Their ways are different, that's all. Yes, Ben remembers and he refers to our father as 'that scary man.'

'Hey, Howie, do you remember that scary man? That scary man who used to live with you, me and Mummy?'

'Sure, Ben.'

'He was scary, wasn't he?'

'Yes, he was, Ben.'

'He was our dad.'

'I think you have to earn the right to be called *Dad*. Let's just call him *that scary man*.'

'Okay, Howie. Okay.'

I would love to say our mother was better – that she understood Ben's autism and that she was caring, loving and nurturing. But she wasn't. Mum – we did call her Mum – was resentful and bitter when our father left. She had to raise us on her own. She couldn't afford proper care for Ben, and back then there wasn't really any proper care anywhere for a child with autism anyway. Things are so much better now. Anyway, my mother never had patience for Ben. She would hit him on the back of the head when he used to parrot words or when he used to do his 'goggle fingers'. And then poor Ben would start rocking back and forth and she would hit him again. I used to stick up for Ben, but it wasn't much good. She would start hitting me. And it hurt. It hurt in lots of ways.

Ben lived with Mum until she died of cancer, some three years ago. I hadn't lived with them since I was eighteen. I couldn't wait to get out of that house, to be honest. I guess I was selfish when I moved out and started living what I thought was a normal life. In those days, in my early twenties, I just wanted to party and get with women and not think about my autistic brother and my bitterly twisted mother. I would go home once a week and every week Ben would greet me with open, forgiving arms. I was his brother and, according to him, I could do no wrong.

I never deserved Ben. I still don't deserve Ben.

When Mum died I had just broken up with Bridget. Or more to the truth, she had just broken up with me. *Bridget*. Bridget the heart-breaker. Oh, she was plump and had the most beautiful smile anyone could possibly have. But I digress. I will come back to Bridget.

Mum had just died, Bridget had moved out of our two-bedroom flat, and it just seemed logical that I would take care of Ben. I'll never forget that day after the funeral when Ben and I drove over to the house he had grown up in, the house I had grown up in, to get his stuff. He said he only wanted his Ted and his art stuff. (Ben is an amazing artist. He can use any medium but I especially like his charcoal drawings, though he does make a mess of himself.)

'Ben,' I said, 'we have to get your clothes. What else?'

'Yes, Howie. Correct. I will need my clothes. No, I don't think there is anything else.'

We walked around the house. I was caught up in a bit of nostalgia, reminding him of the many little things that had happened in that house. He told me that he used to see 'that scary man' sometimes, in dark corners. 'Sometimes in my dreams.'

'There won't be any more of that, Ben. There is no *that scary man* where we are going. It's just you and me, brother.'

'That's right, Howie. You and I are brothers.'

'Always.'

'Always.'

I marvelled at how keen he was to leave the house of his youth. There wasn't one ounce of sentimentality or remorse. He did ask me about Mother:

'Who's going to make Mum's porridge, Howie?'

'You remember we talked about Heaven, Ben?'

'Yeah. Will someone in Heaven make porridge for Mummy?'

'Yes, Ben. Absolutely. And they'll put raisins in her porridge.'

He was delighted and clapped his hands. 'Mummy likes raisins in her porridge.'

And then: 'Can we go now, Howie? I have a lot of arranging to do in my new room. I want my pictures on my walls. I need to colour-code my pencils. I need to put my books in alphabetical order.'

And that was that. You think you know about autism, when you've lived with it long enough. But you never know. They always surprise you. Everything about Ben up until then had always been about order, about routine, about no surprises. But somehow, when it came time to leave his boyhood home, the move didn't seem to bother him at all. They told me at the Mental Health Centre that I would need to quickly establish new routines for Ben, but I was already on top of this. We had our schedule.

I've already relayed bits of our weekly schedule but here's a brief overview, which will fill in the blanks:

Mondays: I work at the Mental Health Centre twelve hours a week. Four hours each day on Monday, Tuesday and Wednesday mornings. They nicknamed me the 'Comfort Man'. Basically, I just hang out with the kids, the same kids every week, and I've become a familiar face for them. I'm not qualified or anything, but the professionals down at the Centre observed me one day, when I was volunteering, and they said I had a calming effect. So they offered me the part-time 'minder' job.

When I'm at work and Ben is at home, I usually let him play video games. He is very good at them. And he becomes so absorbed that he hardly notices I am gone. It somehow works and anyway, he's got his phone and can call me at any time. Sometimes I bring him with me to work. He knows everyone down at the Centre anyway.

We usually go out for a daily, one-hour walk after lunch. We go to the park. Sometimes, if I have some shopping to do or an errand to run, I put his earmuffs on him and we go to the high street.

Late Monday afternoons, Chapstick and I meet and we go record scouring. Sometimes Ben will tag along. (He can look endlessly at the designs of the album covers, particularly if they are drawn or painted.) But more often than not, I leave him at home and set him a task: rearranging my albums or books, or doing the vacuuming. He really loves to vacuum (with the earmuffs on).

Tuesdays after work and the walk, we do housekeeping. Housekeeping can involve actual housekeeping but it can also sometimes lead to gaming the whole afternoon. We then go to the pub for dinner.

Wednesdays are pretty much identical to Mondays. However, if Arsenal has a midweek game at the Emirates, we'll go to that. I don't care much for the late midweek games. They go past Ben's bedtime and he gets sleepy and he gets very angsty after the game when we have to stand in the endless, claustrophobic lines waiting to get on the tube. I am seriously thinking of cancelling mid-week games.

Thursdays Ben and I often take the train out into the countryside and have a daytrip. He really loves it. We go to all sorts of places. We look for quiet places – parks and reserves – where Ben feels safe. It's interesting how wide open spaces comfort him and closed in spaces freak him out. If there wasn't a person on this earth, besides me, I think Ben would be rather happy. Occasionally we go out late in the day, particularly in spring, and we take the telescope. We would do this more often but Ben gets sleepy as the day goes on. And the seeing isn't great until it gets really dark. And in the winters it's too cold. But he does like looking at the moons of Jupiter, say, or the surface of our moon. He always thinks he sees people walking on the moon. Ben does amazing drawings of the moon. They are so accurate it's frightening.

Fridays it's all puzzles and games. In the morning we will do a thousand-piece puzzle and in the afternoons we play FIFA. He always wins, and sometimes that really pisses me off, but I never show him that I am pissed off. The worse thing anyone can do is get angry around Ben. He doesn't understand anger. I think that's how *that scary man* really fucked him up. If you get angry with an autistic person, you must really have issues, you know? Sure, it's frustrating, don't get me wrong, I get frustrated. I can be impatient too. But the last thing in the world I want to do, no matter how I feel, is hurt my brother in any way. (And if anyone else tries to hurt my brother, well, put it this way, I am going to fuck you up.)

We also go to the pub on Fridays and afterwards Chapstick and I head off, either to his place or mine, and we play records. Ben is sometimes with us, but often he is just too tired, so I drop him at home.

The weekend is mostly about football. If there is a home game we'll definitely be going. Ben loves Arsenal as much as I do, and he enjoys going to the Emirates. It is heavy-duty people density, but he's got used to it over the years. As long as we have the same seats and as long as he has his earmuffs, he seems to cope. The first thing I do when we score a goal is hug Ben. I never see him happier than in those moments after the ball has hit the net. And when the opposition scores, Ben usually pats me on the shoulder and says, 'Don't worry, Howie, we'll score again.'

'You're a true gooner, Ben.'

'You're a true gooner, Howie.'

Well, that's the schedule. It is written out, in detail, on a bunch of taped together A4s and stuck to the refrigerator. Ben doesn't spare a detail. He needs the schedule and, to be honest, so do I. It's okay to live life this way. None of my exes would have approved. All three of them talked about adventure and inspiration and spontaneity, and stuff like that. But I don't care anymore what my exes would or would not approve of. Everyone, according to Ben and me, needs a schedule.

* * *

Something happened to us on the way to the Mental Health Centre this morning. I'd like to say it's an odd occurrence but it happens more often than people think. A young man with tattoos, blue hair and a nose-ring sat opposite us on the tube. Curious, Ben couldn't stop looking at him. I tried to avert his eyes, tried to get his focus on the game on his mobile phone but he couldn't stop looking at the young man. Finally the young man snarled and said, 'Oy, are you looking at me?'

'Are you looking at me?' parroted Ben nervously.

'Take it easy,' I said. 'He has autism.'

'Yeah,' said Ben, 'I have autism.' And then Ben did his 'goggle fingers'. This is when he puts his fingers around his eyes, goggle shaped, and he stares at the person or thing that scares him.

The young man, who was about to alight, shook his head. 'You're *well* sick, aren't you?'

'My brother's not sick,' I said firmly. 'He's just different.'

And Ben said quickly, his fingers still shaped like goggles around his eyes, 'The truth? You can't handle the truth!'

Okay, so a few things have happened here. It's all a part of his autism. These things, these things that many consider odd, are simply coping mechanisms for Ben. Nothing unusual, when you think about it. He feels anxious. He reacts. The finger goggles freak people out because Ben just stares intensely at people through the goggles. But I know what he is doing. He's scared, so he puts on his finger goggles as they act as a protector shield. It's as if he becomes a super hero. And then there's the parroting. I guess people don't like it when Ben repeats what they have just said, but it's Ben's way of saying he understands what the other person is doing or saying. It's his way of saying 'I get it'. Lastly, and this is usually his last resort when he is really scared, he says: 'The truth? You can't handle the truth!' I have to take a little responsibility for this one. Some years ago we were watching that old movie *A Few Good Men*. Chapstick was there, watching with us. And then that scene came on and as soon as Ben saw Jack Nicholson delivering those lines, he repeated the phrase. Chapstick and I, well, we started laughing, and Ben said the phrase again. And then we laughed again. It went on and on. And over the years it became a phrase of comfort for him, and then it developed into another of his coping mechanisms. Most people who know Ben are used to him uttering these words. But when he uses it on strangers they are often put off guard. *The truth? You can't handle the truth!* It seems to stop them in their tracks. Honestly, it has become a very useful coping mechanism, and one that I have often thought of using myself. So this morning, as the young man was getting off the tube, I decided to parrot Ben:

'Yeah, you can't handle the truth, buddy!' I said loudly.

The young man had WTF written all over his face. He got off the tube and Ben quickly got back to the game on his phone.

* * *

When we got to the Mental Health Centre we learned that Betty, Ben's long time contact nurse, was off sick, and they didn't know when she would be back. Apparently it's a serious illness, but they weren't privy to telling us more. Well, as you can imagine, this set everything off for Ben. I could feel his anxiety growing.

We were assigned a new contact person. Her name was Zadie and, for all my dealings with the Mental Health Centre, I had never come across her before.

'I used to work with people with Down's,' she said as we entered the room and sat down. 'But I've been on maternity leave and taking care of my young kids for about five years now. So I only just started again this week.'

'Where's Betty?' Ben asked anxiously.

'Betty is sick, Ben.'

'Is she going to die? My mummy died.'

'We don't know yet, Ben. But I promise that when we find out we will tell you first, okay?'

'How do you feel, Ben?' I asked.

'I feel a bit sad,' Ben said, and then he did his goggle fingers.

The first response from Zadie was to try and suppress this urge. She gently took his hands from his face and said, 'Now, we don't do things like that, do we, Ben?'

'We don't stimmy,' Ben replied stiffly, using a long-ago phrase that I was surprised to hear come out of his mouth.

'That's right, Ben. You're a good boy, Ben,' said Zadie.

This was awful. This was wrong. What was this woman doing? Why would she want to take away his coping mechanisms? When Ben immediately reverted to his goggle fingers again, she again smiled and gently removed his hands from his face.

'The truth? You can't handle the truth!'

I got him out of the room and went up to the desk, where Marsha, the head of the Centre, stood over her paperwork.

'Oh hi, Howie,' she said. 'Hello Ben. My word you are handsome today.'

Ben smiled and softly took her hand.

'Everything okay?' asked Marsha.

'It's the new woman,' I said. 'I don't think she has done much work with autism.'

'Zadie is fully qualified, Howie. She knows what she is doing. And well, I guess you heard about Betty.'

'She's suppressing his quirks.'

Marsha breathed out. It was probably the last thing she needed, me complaining. 'Everyone has their ways, Howie. I know you think you know it all, but you've got a lot to learn, Howie. Sometimes I think you think you know better than everyone else.'

'This isn't about me.'

'Isn't it?'

We went back and let Zadie do a check-up on Ben. We had to.

Every month they need to rubber stamp my caring. So we really had no choice. By the time Zadie had finished, Ben was in a flux. He was repeating everything Zadie was saying.

'You're healthy, Ben.'

'You're healthy, Ben'

'You're very smart, Ben.'

'You're very smart, Ben.'

'You're repeating every word I say, Ben.'

'We don't stimmy! Silly Ben!'

Zadie smiled, as if she was actually getting somewhere with Ben. As if she'd just had a victory. She looked at me smugly, and then back at Ben.

'Your brother is taking good care of you, Ben, isn't he?'

When she said this Ben looked at me and said: 'My brother is the best person in the world.'

* * *

Later on, I took him to the pub. I asked him where he wanted to go and that's what he said, the pub. Just to be clear, Ben doesn't drink alcohol. He drinks coke, and after two cokes I tell him he can't drink coke anymore. He also likes cranberry juice. But he likes the pub. He knows everyone there, and they know him. It's not a place of surprises. There's a big screen that plays the football. There are the pool tables out back. (Ben likes a game of pool and often plays with retired fireman Browny. Browny is sweet with Ben. He answers all sorts of crazy questions about fire-trucks.) And then there's Bea, who, right away, as we entered the pub, asked Ben if he wanted a game of chess.

'Yes, I do,' answered Ben politely. 'I very much do.'

But now, let me digress a little, because, well, Chapstick and Pontiac were already at it when I came over to them with a few pints. And well, I think it's a really interesting digression. Chapstick was waxing a theory, and a pretty good one at that:

'There isn't one original genre, or sub genre, of music since 1975.'

We'd touched on 1975 before, stating our favourite albums of that year: *Blood on the Tracks, Born to Run, Marcus Garvey, Horses and Nighthawks at the Diner,* but this was a new idea, and I liked where Chapstick was going. 'Go on,' I said.

'Hang on,' said Pontiac. 'Not sure I'm buying this one. 'What about hip-hop? Just one example that immediately comes to mind.'

'That rings true,' I added. 'And how about electronica? House? Dance? Madchester? Grunge?'

'Okay. Okay,' said Chapstick, smiling. 'So what if I was to say that *fusion* doesn't count? Isn't hip-hop something like funk or rhythm and blues fused with rap? I'm just saying, all those elements were already in place well before 1975. As for electronica, well, is it true to say it's original just because it's synthesized or computerized? Its structure, the chord changes – not new really, is it? It's the same shit, just wrapped in different colours. That goes for pretty much everything else, I reckon. Nothing original about grunge or madchester. Nothing.'

'Not bad,' I said nodding. 'Not bad at all.'

'What about punk?' said Pontiac defiantly.

'There's no such thing as punk music,' said Chapstick. 'Punk is an attitude. It's not a musical form. Certainly not an original one, anyway.'

'What about Radiohead?' I said. 'Aren't they original?'

'No, they're just good. Really good.'

'And getting better. Their last three records are the best they've put out.'

'No chance,' said Pontiac. '*OK Computer.* I think you'll find that Rolling Stone Magazine and its millions of readers agree with me.'

'RSM – the home of the haughty!' I declared and Chapstick nodded and laughed eagerly.

'I'm afraid,' mumbled Pontiac stoically, bringing the conversation to a sudden close, 'we'll have to agree to disagree on that one.'

It usually goes on like that, and those kinds of conversations can continue for hours. I am not kidding. But just for the record, and just to clear things up, Pontiac is wrong about Radiohead. *OK Computer* is not their best record. Fact. When Pontiac leaves, Chapstick and I usually have to go over our conversation, just to make corrections like that. But it's all good. Pontiac is a nice guy, and, as said before, he does come up with some of his own good theories now and then.

* * *

Anyway, it had been a long day. When Ben and I got home that night there was a programme on TV he insisted on watching. He'd heard about it down at the Centre. But, as it was getting past his bedtime, I asked him if he wouldn't prefer to hit the hay?

'This programme is about people with autism, Howie.'

We sat down and watched, Ben with a glass of milk and me with a dram of whisky.

The show is called *Love Is Mental*. It's a show where the producers arrange dates between disabled people, and then they film the dates in all their awkwardness, and, sometimes, hilarious sincerity. Some of the subjects have autism, some of them Down's syndrome, and there are various other mental disabilities and people with learning difficulties. At first I thought the show was taking the piss out of disabled people and I wondered if they weren't being offensive, but, just looking at Ben riveted to the television, it was a revelation.

'You like this, Ben?'

Ben didn't answer. When I laughed at a few awkward moments into one of the dates, Ben just looked at me sternly.

When the show finished Ben looked at me and declared: 'Howie, I want to be on that show!'

'Why would you want to be on the show, Ben? It's embarrassing, isn't it? Do you want to embarrass yourself?'

'Howie,' he said, and I could see a fire burning in his eyes, 'I want to be on the TV show.'

'Why?'

'Because I want to fall in love, Howie. I want it to be just like the movies.'

'It's never like the movies, Ben. Trust me. I know.'

'You don't know, Howie. You have failed at all your love affairs.'

'That's a bit harsh. I just haven't found the right partner, that's all.'

'*I* haven't found the right partner, Howie.'

'You want a girlfriend?'

'I want to fall in love, Howie. I want to have a girlfriend and a wife and children.'

'You're jumping a little ahead of yourself, Ben.'

'I'm not you, Howie. If I have a wife, I will give her everything she ever wanted. I will do my best, every day, every hour, every minute to make her happy and safe and beautiful. I will make her happy, Howie.'

'Okay, Ben.'

'You can't stop me, Howie. I want to fall in love. I want to be on that TV show.'

'Okay, Ben.'

'I am going to bed now, Howie. And in the morning we are going to call that TV show. I am going to fall in love, Howie. This is my chance. I am going to get married and have children.'

He walked off to bed.

I turned the TV off and sat in silence. I kept hearing in my head what he said: *I'm not you, Howie. I will do everything for my girlfriend.* He would too. He would be a marvellous boyfriend.

That's true. But where did this all leave me? I sat and pondered, and as I pondered I couldn't help but think about love and where it all had gone wrong for me. Why had my relationships all fallen apart? I loved those women. I loved them so much. It's true, I wasn't prepared to do everything for them, but I still did a lot. I tried, didn't I?

It crushed me when they left. Each time, a solid mind-fucking crushing.

I checked my stargazing app and it said that Venus was out to the northeast. It was high enough above the horizon that it should be visible. I went to the window but all I could see was the pink-hue clouds of a sticky London. I wished, against all logic, I could see clearly. And then a mental check: I wished I was a better person.

3

I said earlier that I had only three interests. Well, that's not entirely true, if you include the opposite sex as an interest. Does that count? It's an interest that sprouted, with the beginnings of patchy pubic hair, in my early teens and, to be honest, it's an interest that plagues me to this day. And now I struggle with the idea that I have a so-called interest that *plagues* me. I don't know how to classify women, exactly. It's not like I can categorize them, like I do my albums or my books. And it's not like I can file them away, or put them in the garage thinking I'll get back to that hobby one day. They are ever-present. They walk the streets. They sit in the parks. They laugh. Their skin is smooth. They come in all shapes and sizes and I love them all. Okay. Okay. I don't love them all. I have types. But in any case, on any given day, in this big city, you can pretty much find my type anywhere and everywhere. In every nook and cranny. And, yet, when it comes to holding one of these beauties, to loving one, to being loved by one, they are so elusive. In all my years, I've only struck gold three times, and all three times the gold turned to dust and blew with the wind from the very palms of my hands. In all three cases I had no choice about breaking up. In all three cases they told me they loved me, 'but...'. And then they walked out the door.

Just for the record, I don't think of women as 'things' – things to look at, or things to have sex with, or things to cook dinner or clean my apartment. I know women are, for the most part – barring a few lumps and some hairy areas – essentially the same as men. I mean, fuck all that *Venus and Mars* crap – we're the same species, aren't we? And I believe in equality, I really do. But at the same time, I just can't help but get confounded by them. I'm all pent up with longings, needs and wants. Everything I desire seems to be wrapped up in their dresses, like a delicious burrito. There I go again. It's a subject that is circular and has no end – no explanation, no conclusion, and no resolution. So I don't know if it counts as an interest. I only know that my interest in them has never waned. And sometimes it borders on obsessive.

Just as a sidebar, Chapstick and I decided some years ago that we weren't going to be those mates that go on and on about women: talking about who we fucked or didn't fuck or who we want to fuck. Having said that, as far as I can gather, neither of us have had sex in some years. We are the utterly fuckless. Although, then again, we don't talk about it, so how would I know? Chapstick's all right. He once told me that he was done with women and I completely understand that sentiment. It is nowhere near the truth, but I completely understand that sentiment.

I guess I thought it was all about sex in the beginning. It seemed to be. I was eighteen when I met Anna and she and I had so much sex that some mornings I had to peel skin off my penis, just so we could do it again. She was insatiable. And she would do anything. She taught me everything I know and to this day (well, more accurately till three years ago) I've been using the same tricks. Thank you for that, Anna.

Anna was small and mousy. She had brown hair and she had a doll's face. She had the craziest dimples when she smiled. I suppose she was slightly chubby. Her breasts were enormous. I loved them, deeply. I joked that the three of us, her tits and I, might run away. She had the smallest hands but she could do anything with them. I don't mean just sexually. I mean that she was very handy and had a way of fixing things. She was efficient, and that was just as well, because I was thoughtless and single-minded and I didn't really care about anything as long as she was there, in my bed every night.

We moved in together when we were eighteen. Anna was training to be a nurse. For all I know she is one now, working at some hospital, taking care of people and no doubt fixing things. She is probably a boss. A head nurse I would reckon. She was awfully bossy.

At that stage of my life I had decided I was going to be a teacher, so I was going to Teacher's College. Of course this was short-lived, but it was what I was attempting during the time I was with her. I also worked part-time in a pub. We got by, thanks largely to Anna's parents who decided, as long as we were enrolled and studying, they were happy to take care of our rent. They weren't rich or anything. They were well working class. But they had hopes for Anna and they really liked me. They were happy to help.

This arrangement did eventually lead to complications, once I dropped out of Teacher's College. We didn't tell Anna's parents right away. We just went on letting them pay the rent. Not a very nice thing to do really. But I blame her for that. She took control of that situation. She always took control. That was the thing about Anna: as long as she had control everything was fine. And for the most part, I went along with this. I was happy to be controlled.

Anna didn't really share my interests in football or music. She liked it when I talked about space and she used to laugh when I imitated Sagan, 'billions and billions,' but, for the most part, she didn't mind what interests I had. If I was at the football, she was at the gym or having coffee with a friend. If Chapstick and I were out looking for records, Anna would be at a bookshop, or drinking with her buddies. It was okay to be different. She thought it was what made us a good couple.

We lived together for four years. In the first two years of that relationship I must have had sex, or so it felt, at least twice a day. Don't think I'm joking. It was crazy. After the first two years, however, my interest in sex with her began to wane. Or perhaps my other interests began to refocus. Why have sex when I can watch the new Marvel movie? Why have sex when I can listen to a podcast about Arsenal? Why have sex when I can masturbate to online pornography? Okay. There it is. I suppose my sexual drive hadn't waned at all. I guess, after years of the same thing, as great as she was in the sack, I was losing interest in her and her body.

What happens when that happens?

By this time she was working as a fully-fledged nurse and I was working full-time in a bar. It was nice when our shifts aligned, but on those weeks when she was working days, well, it got to us barely seeing each other. She was also losing patience with me. Was I lazy? Was I unambitious? Was I idling? For fucks sake, I was only twenty years old. In any case, she was moving forward in life, and, well, I seemed to be stagnant. I kept saying I was going to go back to studying but I just didn't know what to study. I just hadn't found my direction, my vocation, my calling.

And here's an odd thing, all the time I was with Anna, she only met my brother, Ben, and my mother once. This was something I was unaware of until she pointed it out later. Was I ashamed of them? Was I embarrassed? I don't know. All I know is that between eighteen and twenty-two I rarely went home. I suppose I was just breaking free. Anyway, I was quick to move back in with Mum and Ben when Anna left me. I was there in a flash. And I was in pieces.

It's hard to say what went wrong. I could point out all of the things she said when we broke up, but I don't think anyone speaks with clarity when they break up. My sexual interest in her waned, as I said, and as that happened I think I became even more obsessed with things like music and football and hanging out with Chapstick. Did I neglect her? Probably. But I was too young to understand that a relationship is work. Not all work, of course. Plenty of play too. But in the end, you do need to work on the play to make it work. I am not sure I did that. I think *she* tried. In the end she kept suggesting things we could do together, but by that time I just assumed she was always going to be there and that I didn't have to worry about doing things with her. I could do what I wanted and she would be there to comfort me when I got home. That was what I thought.

She met someone else.

I didn't, and I don't, blame her. She met someone who started telling her how beautiful she really was (and she was!). He told her about what life could be like and that they could travel and they could go out dancing and they could experiment with drugs. He told her he would do all the things that I wasn't prepared to do. Travel? Why? (I would miss too many games.) Dance? I have a theory about dancing. Dance music is another beast to what I would call *real* music. This theory goes something like: If you like music you can dance to, you probably don't like real music. One can't dance to 'Strawberry Fields Forever' or 'Like a Rolling Stone', or 'Flamenco Sketches'. Now that I think of it, I might have to revive this theory. It's one that Chapstick and I have discussed, but I am sure Pontiac hasn't heard it. As for the last element on her life-could-be-like-that list, drugs, well, I don't know why drugs terrify me, but they do. I have this idea that if I take drugs, I am going to fall off the edge of the planet. I will go crazy. Mental. I'll lose my shit.

I was shattered, to say the least, when Anna left. I tried my hardest to get her back. There was a lot of crying. To her credit, she cried a lot too. She told me that she did love me, but that it was time to move on, for both of us. She said that I would understand one day and I would appreciate the fact that she let me go. She told me it was the best thing for both of us.

It wasn't the best thing for me. It was the fucking worst thing possible for me. I moved back in with Mum and Ben, I quit my job and for a while I even stopped going to Highbury. (Those were peak Arsenal years too. How on earth did that happen?) I acquainted myself with the foetal position and lay in it for hours at a stretch. On the floor, just looking at the floorboards.

Dribbling between the cracks in the floorboards. I would listen to sad songs and insisted at that time that only sad songs were permitted. Here are the ones that got heaviest rotation:

'Sarah' by Bob Dylan.

'Sitting on the Dock of a Bay' by Otis Redding.

'If You Could Read My Mind' by Gordon Lightfoot.

'Sunday Morning Coming Down' by Kris Kristofferson.

'She's Gone', by Hall & Oates (just to be clear, not a Hall & Oates fan, but this song: whoa!).

'I Just Don't Think I'll Ever Get Over You' by Colin Hay.

'Tears of a Clown' by Smokey Robinson & The Miracles.

'Waitin' Around to Die' by Townes Van Zandt.

Chapstick stopped coming over for a few weeks. But when he finally did come over, he said, 'You've got to snap out of this, Howie. When you're up for playing something cheerful, something like "This Charming Man" or "The People Who Grinned Themselves to Death", then we can move forward.'

But Chapstick wouldn't know this breakup feeling, not for another ten years or so. That's right, he went out with a beautiful lady called Melinda for thirteen years total, but of course they inevitably broke up. He said, when the time came, it was a mutual decision, but he was shattered. (You didn't want to play happy songs then, did you, Chapstick?)

Chapstick and I have had many arguments over 'best breakup album' and we have narrowed it down to two: *Blood on the Tracks* (of course) and *The Boatman's Call.* As much as I love Dylan, I love *The Boatman's Call* so much I can't bear to listen to it. It's the greatest breakup album ever. Unlistenable. *Fact.* (Special updated mention to *For Emma, Forever Ago,* which wasn't released yet for my first two breakups.)

It took ages to get over Anna. I was always afraid of bumping into her, or seeing her with her new boyfriend. But it never happened. That disparity of interests kept the likelihood of us coming across each other to a minimum. I did meet her years later, but by that time I was already dating Carrie.

* * *

There's no doubt about it, Carrie was a completely different kettle of fish. How do I explain Carrie? The woman who holds the long distance (of being with me) record? I was with her for six whole years.

We met at a Radiohead concert. She stood out, being tall and goofy looking. Don't get me wrong, she may have looked goofy, but she was super intelligent. I mean crazy smart. And I think she was really good looking too, in an Irish way. She had beautiful skin (freckly in the summer) and big blue eyes. Her hair was brown but in the sunshine it took on a hue of ginger. It was short, cut flat and straight around her neck. She had a perfectly straight-cut fringe. I really loved her face. I loved to hold it in my hands when I told her how much I loved her. I didn't do that at the Radiohead concert, of course. We were standing next to each other and she kept smiling at me until I asked her if she thought that maybe Thom Yorke was really a lizard, or some kind of alien, or both? For some reason she thought this was funny and she let me buy her a drink.

I don't know what she saw in me. I'm not great looking, although I'm not that bad either. I think my nose is too big, but otherwise I'm kind of normal. I do have a charm, I suppose. It might not sound like it but I can be funny. It's a mechanism I use, of course, particularly around women. When I don't know what to say, I'll say something weird, funny, or I'll do something stupid. It's a clumsy charm, I suppose. It's worked three times. Not to say I haven't slept with women other than Anna, Carrie and Bridget, but there haven't been many others. And I can't recall any one-night-stands or short-term flings that had any type of long-standing meaning for me. I guess I'm a long-term guy. A long-term lover. I really do believe that making love is a learned thing. You get better at it the more you do it with the same person. But I digress, again...

I'm not a dimwit either (despite all appearances). I can talk about things other than space, music and football. For example, Carrie was into art and I had read a book about the history of art. I proclaimed myself to be very interested in the impressionists (but not really that interested) and this so-called interest developed towards the post-impressionists and then on to artists like Picasso and Braque and then Matisse. I'm pretty good at picking out pieces by particular artists. Carrie was impressed with that on our first date at the Tate. As for her, she was into Romanticism. She particularly liked the Pre Raphaelites.

It's worth pointing out that, at this stage, I'd started to do day trips with Ben at least once a week. We'd often go to the galleries. He loved the art but he also loved the peacefulness. Art galleries, museums and libraries, for obvious reasons, have a calming effect on my brother. And if I thought I was good at picking out the work of certain artists, well, Ben was encyclopaedic about it. He recognized styles, periods, movements and he could go home and imitate them. My brother's sense of visual art is astounding, even Carrie said so.

It was also about this time that I started working part-time down at the Mental Health Centre. This was something about me that Carrie came to admire. And she loved my brother, Ben. She encouraged me to bring him along on dates. She was a good person. I don't think Ben liked any of my girlfriends the way he liked Carrie. She really had time for him.

Carrie worked as a graphic designer and she was really good. She even used Ben's drawings in a promotional piece she did for a magazine once. It was amazing to see it in print. Ben had it framed and put on his wall.

So, at first, Carrie found me interesting. She believed that I had varied interests and to be honest, I was a willing participant in most of the things she wanted to do. We went to a lot of gigs. Not always bands that Chapstick or I approved of, but we went anyway. Carrie and Melinda really hit it off too, so it was great, for a while, the four of us hanging out. We were very active, vital, and there seemed to be a future.

Carrie wasn't particularly physical. She wasn't like Anna. She liked sex but she couldn't come unless she used her own fingers. We'd always get her to come first, me entering usually from behind, and she massaging her own clit. She'd come and then she'd let me hop on top, missionary, and I'd come quickly after that. It fell into this routine. After about six months or so, we were down to doing it about once a week. We agreed that that was plenty for us. We agreed, somehow, that we weren't the types that did it like rabbits. Still, any chance I got, I was jerking off to porn on the internet. I'm not proud of it, but I'm not ashamed of it either. It seemed to work. Our relationship seemed balanced and lacked any nuance that might upset things. It was okay.

She was ambitious and she was getting better and better at her job. She began to wear designer clothes and, over the course of a couple of years, she was reinventing herself. She started making new friends. The bands she wanted to see became more and more esoteric and, well, some of them just plain bad. She didn't like the romantics anymore and even Picasso was passé to her. She was thinking more and more about contemporary art and certainly modern design. In any case, I began to not recognize her.

And the more she became different, the more I dug into my sameness, my normality, my humdrum. I started going to the football more, I started clogging up our living room with literally thousands of albums and I bought a very big telescope that I set up by a window in the spare bedroom. It was relatively useless as I could rarely see anything through the London atmosphere. But it was too big to take out to the countryside. I had to settle for, on those crystal clear occasions, studying the moon's surface. The first time I got it focused on the moon I ran and got Carrie and, for a few minutes, a glass of red in her hand, she marvelled at the moon. 'Wow!' she said. 'That's beautiful.' But she never looked through that telescope again.

The more I write these things the more I get incensed about what she said, that day, when she told me I had no interests. The extended version conversation went something like this:

'What do you want to do, Howie? You can't just sit here and do nothing. You work at the bar and at the Mental Health Centre, but don't you want to break out and do something? You're so smart. You're really brilliant. Can't you put your mind to something? Write a book or something? You could write a book about music.'

'I have a theory about overrated underrated bands, do you want to hear it?'

'I want to hear you typing, or doing, or just being enthusiastic.'

'What do you mean?'

'You have no interests, Howie.'

'That's not true.'

'Well, you look into space. Think about that. You look into *space.*'

'An interest if you ask me.'

'It's space, Howie. By definition, it's nothing.'

'There are planets and suns…'

'And music. You say it's an interest, but you like to talk about it, you barely even listen to it.'

'That's not fair.'

'And don't get me started on the football. That's not an interest, that's a dumb-ass lifestyle.'

'You're being pedantic, don't you think? You're choosing your own definitions of things.'

'All I am saying, Howie, is that you're wasting your talents and your skills. You have something to offer. Don't you think so? Don't you think you have something to offer the world?'

Carrie also left me for another guy. It wasn't long after that conversation. I think she finally got fed up with me. She said I was stagnating.

'There's nothing wrong with being stagnant,' I said. 'Creatures aren't born flowing down a river.'

'Creatures aren't meant to sit still. Some of them die if they don't move. You're clinging, Howie. You're clinging to a rock.'

'It's a choice.'

'Well, Howie, it's time for me to let go.'

I don't remember if the conversation went exactly like that, but I do remember the metaphor of river creatures being used. I wonder, right now as I write this, am I still clinging to that same rock? Is that my life?

No. No. No. I don't think so.

I think it's worth skipping the heartbreak part with Carrie, because it was pretty much identical to my breakup with Anna. I moved home to Mum. I wallowed in self-pity and this time it lasted for years. You get older, right? Let me tell you, in case you don't know, breakups become harder as you get older. They really do. There's an added gravitas there. Will I ever meet someone? Will I spend the rest of my life alone? Is it over for me? Did I blow it? And then you look in the mirror and you notice the crow's feet and the grey hair and you start fucking crying because you know, beyond any shadow of a doubt, that you will never, ever, ever fall in love again. You're done.

There's also the fear. Let's not forget the fear. The fear of losing again. The fear of feeling that debilitating heartbreak again. It not only gets overwhelming to think you'll never meet anyone again, or fall in love again, but a part of you thinks: I don't want to! I can't! I won't go through all that pain again. I won't survive another breakup.

* * *

3

And that brings me to Bridget. Lovely Bridget.

Bridget and I met at the football, which, when I think about it, was the perfect setup. If she was into the Arsenal, surely I'd met my perfect woman, right?

Bridget always said that Arsenal was her team, but she wasn't really into football. Not like me anyway. When we'd lose, she'd say things like: 'Why are you so upset? It's only a game honey.' Well, it's true, it *is* only a game. Only it isn't. It's upsetting to lose, especially to Chelsea, Man U or Spurs. But she was never upset about losing. In retrospect, that's very suspicious. Was she really a fan, or just faking it? And what else was she faking?

Ben just pointed out to me that the game she attended, when I met her, we won. We beat Liverpool. A right whomping of them in fact. A very good day. Bridget was there on her Aunty Karin's (aka Badger) ticket. She was so enthusiastic, laughing and yelling and trying to sing along. She had an Arsenal scarf around that lovely neck. Her eyes were hazel and her hair was black. Her face was long and skinny and her nose was cute and kind of pointy. Ah, I paint an awful portrait, don't I? She was lovely in every single way. I was drawn to her immediately. I would have got nervous if we were in a bar, but we were at the Arsenal and they were popping in goals for fun. We even hugged when we scored our second goal. She smelled of musk. I wanted to kiss her right there and then.

In the joy of celebrations I managed to ascertain that she was single and I dared to ask her out. It had been around eighteen months since Carrie and I had gone our separate ways, so it was time, I reckoned. Anyway, I don't know how I got up the courage, but I did it. Bridget just smiled and said, 'Sure, let's go out.'

And thus began what I would call my number one, gold record, Halley's comet relationship. It wouldn't be the longest lasting, it wouldn't be the most sexual, but it would turn out to be the most fulfilling and the most satisfying. Bridget, more than anyone, taught me things about myself and about life. It wasn't an intellectual thing. I simply observed her. She was an exceptional human being, and I wanted that too. I also wanted to be exceptional. And for a very short time, a very short time indeed, I did feel exceptional. I really did. I was proud to be with Bridget. I was, for a moment in time, proud to be me.

We moved in together some six months after we met. It seemed right at the time, for both of us. Bridget worked at an IT firm. I never really understood exactly what she did, but for the next few years, if there were any problems with any of the many gadgets in the house, Bridget would know how to fix them. She was brilliant. But she was so much more than a tech whizz. She liked the movies I liked, we liked all the same music (not kidding!) and she enjoyed, so she said, watching and supporting Arsenal. She was also an avid reader and she also managed to push me into a new and unlikely interest: she got me reading poetry.

She was quick to point out Rimbaud, and the many references Dylan had made to the great French poet. Also, the influence of Ginsberg and the beat poets on Dylan. But she also got me interested in Baudelaire, and Dylan Thomas, and Pablo Neruda and E.E. Cummings, and many more. So, if you think about it, I really have four interests. (Although this one, Carrie, came after you.) Or had. The solemn truth is I haven't read a word of poetry (outside of Dylan's lyrics, and there's many arguments out there as to whether that's poetry or not) since Bridget left. I can't. That part of me was for her, so when she left my life, so did the poetry.

It was strange and incredible to be with someone that was so in tune with my life, in tune with my likes and dislikes, who liked the same kind of food, who was as messy as me, and who had no interest in controlling me. Everything seemed to be right. I really loved her and I felt that she loved me. It was too perfect, really.

We had good sex too. It wasn't prolific, like with Anna, but it was good. In the first year or so we tried out some new things and generally we could laugh in bed, laugh at each other, and laugh at how funny sex really was, when you thought about it. And that leads me to her great sense of humour. Or should I say, her penchant for laughter. That's what I remember most about Bridget – her laughing. She seemed to be always laughing. And her face lit up like a ferris wheel when she laughed. It was like flicking a switch. Her face was the very essence of joy.

But humour is a funny thing. No pun intended. Now, looking back, it was always me generating the humour. It was always my jokes. I don't remember Bridget ever telling a joke. But boy could she laugh at them. It was very gratifying to be with someone that thought all my jokes were funny. It was like I was her very own personalized, stand-up comic. It was brilliant, come to think of it.

It was around the time my mum was diagnosed with cancer that I proposed to Bridget. I can't remember what came first. All I remember is that the proposal triggered the downfall of our relationship, and that was oddly parallel with my mother losing her life. It all happened rather quickly.

I took her out to a nice restaurant and I set everything up – the expensive ring, the expensive champagne and the very expensive lobster – and I proposed. I even got down on one knee. But I could tell right away that something was up. She didn't answer. She started hyperventilating. (Subtle tell, I know.) It got so bad that we took her down to the local emergency ward to get her checked out, but it turned out that she was just having a panic attack. A panic attack, I guess, that was triggered by my proposal. I was okay with it all. I didn't blame her. I understood panic attacks because I'd seen Ben have many over the years. But I also naïvely thought that the reaction to my proposal wasn't necessarily a 'no' and that likely she was just overwhelmed by the occasion. I was still sure she would marry me. So at the hospital I asked her again and this time she said flatly, 'No.'

She said that she'd been thinking about 'us' for a long time, and that she was starting to feel a little penned in. She said that we were so alike, that life was taking on a sameness that she was becoming increasingly uncomfortable with. And no, she hadn't met anyone. That hurt all the more, to be honest. This time I was being left, not for someone else, but for *no one* else. She said she wanted to move down to the south coast.

'I love the south coast,' I said. 'I can come with you. I could get a job down there.'

'What about Ben?'

'We could set him up down there, somewhere nearby.'

'Can he live by himself?'

I had to think long and hard on that. But I was desperate, desperate for Bridget not to leave me. 'Yes, sure he can,' I said.

But she shook her head. She didn't want me to come to the south coast with her. She wanted to go by herself. She wanted to start anew.

'I don't understand.' I must have said this a billion times. And the truth is, I never really got an adequate explanation as to why Bridget left me. And that's the worst part about it. She said she couldn't explain. She said that some things can't be explained. All she could tell me was that she *knew* it was the right thing to do.

'Right for whom?'

She left and I was left wondering. And in all of this melee my mother died and Bridget moved out and Ben moved in. I am thankful that Ben moved in. He didn't understand why I was crying all the time, but he would hug me and tell me that everything was going to be fine.

Thank you, Ben. I might not have survived without you.

Bridget was the worst breakup. By far and away it was the one that hurt me most. She was the one that I loved the most, and I still do love her, if it comes down to it. Everything seemed so right. She was the one that I could imagine spending the rest of my life with. She was the one that understood me, and that never pressed me to be anyone but myself. She was the one that finished my sentences, that laughed at my jokes and that listened to a song and said 'that sounds like...' and she was right every time. She was the one that I thought I would grow old with. She was the one that I would die beside. She was the one.

And then there is the no-explanation breakup. So the question hangs: would you rather have someone leave you for someone else, or leave you with no real explanation? What is the best kind of breakup? You think you know, but you don't know till you've met your Bridget.

I wonder what she is doing, right now. Is she laughing? Or is she sad because she left the love of her life? (That's me, by the way.) For about two years I was sure she would see the error of her ways and she would come back to me. But the last time I talked to her on the phone, she told me about how much she loved seaside living. She still wasn't seeing anyone. But she was happy. And she laughed. There was no doubt about it. She was fucking happy. And I was fucking miserable.

Part Two

4

It's now six months since Ben asked me if he could go on the TV show *Love Is Mental.* I'm not sure you could carve out any other period of my life and I would remember it so clearly. The last six months have been utter madness. Mental, if I can borrow that word from the TV show. Now, just to be clear, I'm not proud of what I've done in the last six months. I've made some bad decisions. And I've paid, and am still paying, for those decisions too. I'm still not completely out of the hole I dug for myself. Not in my own mind, anyway. But to all and sundry, I want to apologize in advance for what you are about to read. I should apologize to the whole world. It's fucked up. I'm fucked up. The world is fucked up. But we go on living, don't we? What other choice do we have?

But let me bring things up to date. I'll get to the nitty-gritty soon enough, but first, the constants:

In the last six months, spanning spring through to autumn, Chapstick, Ben and I agree, the Gunners have been pretty shite. It's a particular type of shiteness (awful defending, no creativity, one dimensional) that we as fans have become somewhat used to. But all is not lost. With a few summer signings and a new manager, this new season, things are already beginning to look up. We finished eighth last season, the worst table position in over twenty years, but this season we've beaten Chelsea, United and Leicester (who are pretty good right now). We also lost to Villa and Southampton. Go figure. But anyway, despite everything else that's been going on, things are looking upwards, footballistically.

I've also, again despite recent events, bought a lot of albums, probably more than thirty. Chapstick's probably bought half that many, because he's been distracted (the reason to be later revealed). But anyway, here's a list of the top ten purchases from the last six months, in no particular order:

River: The Joni Letters by Herbie Hancock
The High Country by Richmond Fontaine
Blonde on the Tracks by Emma Swift
The Fallen by Audrey Auld
Stone Flute by Herbie Mann
Àgaetis Byrjun by Sigur Rós
Home by Peter Broderick
Tony Rice Sings Gordon Lightfoot by Tony Rice
Ptah the El Daoud by Alice Coltrane
A Moon Shaped Pool by Radiohead

So these records have been on heavy rotation. But as great as all these records are, there are songs in there that now, as I'm writing, evoke uncomfortable memories. For the most part, memories of me being a dickwad. Chapstick and I have talked many times about the power of music. How songs bring up memories and how they act like postcards or photos. But what if the memory that's being conjured is a bad one? What do we do then? Turn it off, I suppose. And, I hate to keep coming back to Carrie, but, well, how the fuck is it that she thought that listening to music was an intellectual pursuit for me? Clearly it's emotional. In fact, I'm not sure I care for any music that doesn't provoke me in some way emotionally. So, wrong again, Carrie!

Ah! But for fuck's sake, why, in light of everything that's happened, am I thinking of Carrie again? Carrie of all people! She's like a recurring nightmare. Okay. Okay. I did hear, a few months ago, that she was getting married. But that didn't affect me at all. Not at fucking all. Fuck it! Not in the god damn, fucking least. At fucking all! *Cunt!*

Where do I start with everything else? Oh, the TV show. Fucking *Love Is Mental*. That, unfortunately, is where we have to start.

For weeks Ben badgered me to helping him get on that show.

4

I finally relented and I started looking into finding the names and contact details of the producers. It wasn't that difficult really. It turned out that the producers had been visiting the Mental Health Centre, asking for advice and trying to find good candidates for the show. When I asked Marsha about it, she said that she was very sceptical about the whole thing. After all there were already a number of dating agencies about town, specifically working with 'challenged' people. Why did they need to put it on TV? Was that entertainment? Were people making fun of them? Was this one big elaborate joke? They explained to her that it was a good way of educating the masses about people with disabilities. She confided to me that she was unsure. But it wasn't as though she could stop them. They were going to make the show with or without her help. In the end she relented, giving them advice and making suggestions.

'Ben wants to go on the show,' I said to her.

'I thought of Ben,' she said. 'But I thought he might be too sensitive. Does he really want the attention that the TV will bring? I assumed he wouldn't like that. I thought it might provoke attacks.'

'There's this couple with autism on the show, Peter and Stefanie.'

'Yes, I know them. I recommended them.'

'He could see how that worked out. That it was a success. That they fell in love.'

'Well, there's a long way to go with that relationship. But it does look promising.'

'He now thinks that this is the only way it's going to work for him. He thinks he *has to* go on the show, in order to find a girlfriend.'

'Howie, you need to set things straight for him. Peter and Stefanie are the exceptions.'

'I've told him. He's very pragmatic. He knows it could fail.'

He knew it could fail. I was convinced of this. There's

something that a lot of people don't know about people with autism. For the most part, they accept the truth, no matter what form it takes. And no matter how hurtful it is. They accept it. They may react poorly, they may even tantrum, but, as long as it's the truth, they understand it and they take it. And if the truth bares logic – all the better. They accept it and they carry on. Unlike with the rest of us, the truth is often a comfort for them.

Anyway, before I made the call to the producers, I had a long conversation with Ben about being cautious:

'It might not work out,' I said.

'I know, Howie.'

'It's not that easy finding a partner.'

'It's been hard for you, hasn't it, Howie?'

'Yes, I suppose so.'

'What percentage chance do you think there is that I will find my wife on *Love Is Mental*, Howie?'

'I would think it's pretty low, Ben.'

'I think it's about 27%, Howie.'

'Ben, Let's be sensible about this, okay?'

'Okay, Howie, 23% 23.5. Okay?'

'You know I love you, Ben. And you really are such a loveable man. You know I think that, right? And you know that even if you don't find a girlfriend on this TV show, you know it has nothing to do with how loveable you are?'

'I'm on the spectrum, though. I'm different, aren't I, Howie?'

'Well, that's not the issue here, is it? Because a lot of the participants on the show are on the spectrum. In fact, on the show, you won't be different at all.'

'Right.'

'But just because the ones you will date have autism too, it doesn't mean you'll be right for them. Autism isn't personality.'

'Not personality.'

'It's all about chemistry, isn't it?'

'That's right. Like you said before, there are lots of women, but not everyone is suitable for me. I have to find the right one. It's like fishing, isn't it, Howie?'

'Do you remember last summer? When we went fishing?'

'We didn't catch a thing. Not even an old boot, Howie.' Ben chuckled at the thought of catching an old boot.

'That's right. And that was at a fish farm.'

'And this TV show, it's like a fish farm, isn't it, Howie?'

'Well, I guess. An autistic fish farm.'

Ben laughed again to himself and mumbled, 'An old boot.'

This was one of many many conversations where, if I'm honest, I was trying to drag my brother away from the whole idea of going on this show. Another stupid misconception about people with autism is that they don't feel anything, that they are emotionless and they lack empathy. But they feel. They feel a great deal. And that was the seed of my worry. I, more than anyone, understood how much he could get hurt in matters of the heart. So it was natural that I was wary. I didn't want some autistic floosy breaking my brother's heart. That was the last thing I wanted. In fact, the very thought of that broke *my* heart.

When I called, the producers said they'd already started shooting season two and they were full up with subjects for the show. Perhaps, they told me, they could interview Ben for season three, but they weren't going to start prep for that until the following year. And, actually, they couldn't even guarantee there would be a season three. Much depended on the show maintaining its current popularity. So in other words: 'come back to us early next year.'

When I put this to Ben I could see that he was disappointed. But he wasn't inconsolable. There was always season three. And I promised him, if he didn't get on to season three, I said that we would go and have a look at one of the dating agencies. He agreed to all this, and I thought we could, for the time being, leave it at that. But he still wouldn't stop talking about the TV show, and he kept watching it, over and over. He particularly loved the success story of Peter and Stefanie. He would pause the stream, stopping on their faces, and he would just look at them and stare at their faces. I don't know what he was thinking when he did this. I think he just wanted the world to stop for a moment. Maybe that's what he thought love was – something that puts the world on pause. Nothing else matters type of thing. Maybe what he saw in those faces was the absence of anxiety. Perhaps that's what he thought love was.

I wish that were true. That love is the absence of anxiety. But love has always been full of anxiety for me. And anxiety, well, it's the fuel of existence.

I sometimes think about what it would be, to be in Ben's brain. People with autism aren't simple and they aren't stupid. For the most part, apart from varying degrees of behavioural quirks, they aren't that much different to anyone else. If you watch someone with autism long enough, you're going to come to understand that everything they do is completely human and utterly logical. For example, I know some people think that stimming is an odd way to behave, but like I've said before, this is just a way of coping. We all have our ways of coping. We might not show the world what it is, but we all have our ways. And we all feel anxiety. Stimming is just out there, for everyone to see. It's an honest response to a moment of normal everyday anxiety. And that's just it really. Their anxiety is their truth. *The truth! You can't handle the truth!* Honesty is at the heart of all the autistic people I have met. In so many ways, perhaps in every way, a person with autism is so much more honest than the rest of us. That's the difference if you come down to it. They're truly honest, and, more often than not, we're not.

Oh shit and fuck! I wish I could be that honest. I wish I could be more like Ben.

Does Ben see love like a fairy tale? A romantic comedy? A

song? If so, how is that different to the way the rest of us see it? It's a good fucking question. After all, who creates these fairy tales, these films and these songs? People with autism? Well, it's possible, but on the whole I don't think so. It's strange, isn't it? We create fantasy, and yet we so often deny it. Everyone calls a true believer naïve these days.

I am not going to lie, I looked at Ben back then and I thought to myself that this boy was going to get fucked up by this TV show. Surely he didn't understand what he was getting into. He couldn't understand love. Yes, love was a fairy tale to him. 'Ben,' I wanted to say, but didn't, 'you're so naïve. Leave it alone.' But when he said to me, 'Howie, I deserve the right to fall in love,' how was I supposed to respond to that? Say no? No you don't! Fuck off! Of course not. Because we all know the answer to Ben's predicament. He is human. He *does* deserve to fall in love. And he also deserves to find out about love in his own way. He has every right to love, and every right to feel the desperate pain that comes with it. And I bet you, I bet the fucking world, that that TV show *Love Is Mental,* will never show the onset of difficulties coming to every person who signs off on their show, and then has to face reality afterwards. Because, really, as we all know, love is just the beginning of the story. As we know, some fairy tales can get very fucking weird. Some of them end up very badly indeed.

I am waffling, and I apologize for that. I just wanted to express my reservations at the time. I love Ben. It made sense I was trying to protect him. So when the producers told me they didn't have a spot for Ben on the show, I was secretly relieved. I hoped that he would just drop it all, forget about it and just get on with his life. I figured we had a good six months before they would audition for season three. I was counting on him forgetting it all by then. At least, that's what I secretly hoped.

As it turned out, a few days later, all these secret hopes and wishes would be snuffed, dashed, and remitted to history. The producers called back saying that they'd had someone drop out of the show and they were desperate to fast-track someone in. Would Ben be interested in coming in for an interview?

There was no turning back now. And, well, this triggered all the events I'm about to relay. Events that have left me feeling somewhat empty, regretful and disillusioned. But what the fuck, let me just get on with telling the story.

* * *

We were ushered down the hallways of a small TV studio in West London. Ben was wringing his hands a little, but overall it was excitement that was driving him rather than overt anxiety. There was a psychologist on hand, someone I'd met down at the Mental Health Centre – a specialist who they hired to consult on the show. His name was Tom. Along with Tom there was Jerry and Patricia, who were the producers of the show. The producers seemed somewhat stressed and they apologized for this, but everything concerning the show was in a bit of a kafuffle because the person Ben 'might' replace had pulled out so suddenly. It occurred to me that they should have been prepared for this. I mean, Ben has pulled out of so many events last-minute over the years. The anxiety is just too much sometimes. Sometimes the coping mechanisms just aren't enough.

After their original call to set up the meeting, they'd asked me a few questions in private: whether I thought Ben would cope with the show and how interested was he, in finding true love? I answered as honestly as I could. Now that he had this shot, I was going to stand behind him. It was important now, to watch over him and make sure that they would treat him with respect and dignity. By the time we got to the interview room, I realized I was scrutinizing them as much as they were scrutinizing Ben.

4

It turned out that the producers, and the psychologist, were all quite lovely. They were gentle with Ben. They seemed to be genuinely interested in helping Ben find what he was looking for. They were kind, respectful, careful to make him feel comfortable. For the first time since this idea had come up, I started to warm to it.

They sat Ben down. They rolled cameras. Ben was wringing his hands. They started to ask him questions:

'So, Ben,' asked Patricia, 'what do you want more than anything in life?'

'I want Arsenal to win the league because it's been a long time since we won the league and we're a big club who should win the league. Right, Howie?' He swung his head my way.

Patricia took a look at me and smiled. I was sure that she had been through this before, with other candidates for the show. She called me over and asked me if I could stand beside her behind the camera, so it would look like Ben was always talking into the camera. I did so.

'Well, what would you like for *you*, Ben?' she continued. 'Something just for you? Not for Howie and not for Arsenal, but for you?'

'I would like to find a girlfriend and live with her and get married and have children. Like in the movies. I would really like that.'

'Why would you like that, Ben?'

'Because it would make me happy. I would wake up every morning with a big smile on my face and I would look at my wife and tell her how much I love her and how much I will take care of her and do anything for her so that she will be as happy as me.'

'That's beautiful, Ben.'

'What kind of interests do you have, Ben?' asked Jerry, the other producer.

'You mean like hobbies and stuff?'

'Yes.'

'I like to draw and paint. I am very good at drawing and painting. I had a drawing of mine in a magazine once, didn't I, Howie?'

'Yeah, mate.'

'I like being with Howie. I like playing games and doing puzzles with Howie. And on the weekends we go to the football. I like the football, but it gets very loud sometimes. I have earmuffs. I like to go to the pub for dinner and play chess with Bea. I'm good at chess.'

'What does it mean to you, to be on the spectrum?'

'Well, I'm different to most people. It's not bad or anything. It's just that I learn differently, and I cope with things differently. Sometimes I can be overwhelmed.'

'When do you get overwhelmed?'

I could see that he was getting edgy at that moment. Somehow, focusing on his own autism could do this to him sometimes. I suppose there is that dreaded cycle that we all experience. You worry about worry and you become more worried. In this case, talking of being overwhelmed was making Ben overwhelmed. I have to say, they handled it brilliantly. It surprised me. They really did seem to understand and they showed they knew what to do. Patricia stood up, poured a glass of water and she took it over to Ben. She didn't even ask him if he wanted it, but he took it and drank it all in one gulp. She smiled at him and he took her hand softly and I could see that he already trusted her. I can't say enough how important this was to me.

She came back and Jerry was smart enough to let Patricia take over the questions:

'Where do you see yourself in ten years, Ben?'

'Living with my wife. Maybe having children. But I don't know. It would depend on my wife and it would depend on whether or not we could handle that. But that would be good. To have children.'

'What about your brother, Howie? You live with your brother now, don't you?'

'I wish for Howie to also be married and happy and in love, and I wish for him to have all the things that I want to have because Howie is a good man. He takes care of me. But we won't live together then. I don't want Howie to have to take care of me forever. I want Howie to be the happiest person alive.'

I had to excuse myself. With the excuse of going to the toilet, which I did, despite not needing to, I rushed off, went into a cubicle and I started crying. I have cried a lot in my life. Too much I reckon. But this was different. Was it joy? Relief? Desperate sadness? Heart-wrenching loss, again? What the fuck was it? I don't want to pre-empt too much, but just a warning – I've cried a lot in the last six months and, for the most part, I have absolutely no clue as to why. Crying is like that sometimes. I think we need to cry. I've said that to Ben many times. 'Don't worry, buddy. We all need a good cry now and then.'

So I wasn't there when they asked him the last question, but some time later, when the show was aired, I saw the question and his response:

'Last question, Ben,' said Patricia, off screen. 'What is love to you?'

'Love is when you will do anything for the other person and you tell them you love them all the time because you can't help it. It's when you think about that person all the time and you want to take them to dinner and you want to tell them how beautiful they are when they get ready and you tell them things like: oh, you've lost weight lately, and you say things like that even if they are not true because love makes you a bit crazy and stuff. It makes you crazy, but in a good way.'

'Thank you, Ben. That's perfect.'

* * *

I've got to make a confession. After I met the producers and Ben got accepted on to the show, I started looking at *Love Is Mental* in a completely different way. It's not that I was initially all negative. I was, perhaps, a little sceptical. But, I don't know, it just took me a while to understand it, and to understand what an impact it could have, and, for all intents and purposes, was having.

I had to watch the show's episodes on my own. In the beginning I liked watching the show with Ben, but then it started to hit me on a new level. It started to have an emotionally transforming effect on me. Like a switch was being turned on inside me. I started to cry uncontrollably when I watched the show. I come back to what I said before when I alluded to uncontrollable and inexplicable crying. I would watch the show, at least once a day, and without fail it would make me cry. What was wrong with me? Did I want to cry? Is that why I kept going back to it? Just to be clear, this didn't impact the rest of my day. In fact, I could argue that it made my days somehow better, happier and more meaningful. It was almost as if my daily crying (or nightly to be more precise) was enabling the happier me to surface elsewhere. Even Chapstick noticed I was happier. I said it was down to Ben and the show. I was happy because Ben was happy.

And Ben *was* happy. As they had planned to, and as they were already shooting, Ben was fast-tracked into the season two narrative. They did a few interviews with us at home (I had to do a lot of cleaning and sorting of stray albums) and then they arranged some dates for Ben. Ben was chuffed, but nervous. He knew that he had to do the dates on his own (or at least without me being there) but somehow Patricia had really won his trust. He often held her hand as she guided him around the cameras. Anyway, Ben's dates, in chronological order, went something like this:

Date 1: This was Olga. Olga was an immigrant from Eastern Europe. (I can't remember which country.) For all intents and purposes, she seemed, like Ben, to cope with her autism and it didn't show that much. Sometimes I think the worst is when someone has autism, but it's mild enough that they come across as being 'normal' but to a so-called 'normal' person they just seem stupid. I can't tell you how many times people have called Ben stupid. It used to incense me, but now Ben and I simply reply: 'It's autism, stupid! Get your facts right! Stupid. Yeah, that's right, you're the one that's stupid!' And then: 'The truth! You can't handle the truth!'

But back to Olga. Olga had a very stiff posture. Her hair was sandy white and her face was often still, until her huge toothy smile came out. Ben thought that she was pretty and I had to agree. I really hoped it might work out with Olga.

According to Ben and the producers, and what I saw later on TV, it was an awkward dinner. We'd tried to coach Ben about how to act during the dinner. And apparently Olga was coached too. But somehow they couldn't strike up a decent conversation, and embarrassment caused more embarrassment, which led to anxiety on both sides. There was one strange moment when Ben asked Olga what she liked. She said she liked gaming and then Ben asked her if she liked a few games he was into. He named them one by one and she just shook her head. She then named another game, very similar, in my opinion, to one of the games Ben mentioned, which she said she liked. Later, being interviewed on her own, she said that she and Ben didn't share any interests. I thought that was a bit rough. But then, I guess she was right, if one was to be ultra specific.

I felt for him when they were saying goodbye outside the restaurant:

'Goodbye, Olga.'

'Goodbye, Ben.'

'So, do you want to do this again?'

'I don't know.'

'Wasn't romantic enough, I suppose.'

'I think we can be friends.'

'Yes, I suppose so,' said Ben. 'Goodbye, Olga.'

And later, on his own, he said this to the camera:

'She just wanted to be friends. It's okay. It's nice to have a new friend.'

But I could see the disappointment on his face. I think he really liked Olga.

The second date was with Wendy. Wendy had very long black hair. She had a round face and nice blue eyes. I was impressed by her sense of humour and her bright smile. Ben also found Wendy very attractive. But, although the date with Wendy was livelier and more comfortable, it ended similarly to the one with Olga. I was very disappointed for him, again, but I was doing my best to keep his spirits up.

'Wendy was very cute,' he told me after the date. 'I really liked Wendy.'

'That's okay, mate. It's like we said, remember, that sometimes it's not the right fish.'

'That's right, Howie. Sometimes you have to put the fish back.'

But I was already getting a little anxious for him. There was that part of me, in the back of my mind, that felt: how dare they reject my brother! And then going on to tell myself that he was too good for them anyway. It's odd, all these thoughts that go through your mind in such instances. It's a kind of *fuck you, everyone*! 'My brother is too good for you all!' And you know it's the cynic in you. It's the ego in you. It's all the bad things inside of you that drive you to that kind of jealousy and anger. The truth is that Ben felt none of this. He accepted everything at face value. They told him that they didn't feel romantically towards him, and he just accepted it and got on with things. 'Maybe the next one, Howie. Maybe the next one!'

And, thankfully, the next one was a hit. It was Robyn. And Robyn, what can I say? I think she was really pretty, and really funny and really, really smart. But there's a lot to say about Robyn. So much. Robyn was the one that changed everything, forever. Yes, change, but perhaps not in the way you would think...

5

Robyn was the epitome of cute, whatever that is. She was medium height, she had a slightly chubby – perfect in my opinion – body and she had big cheeks that dimpled irresistibly when she smiled. And she smiled often. She had the eyes of an optimist. Everything she said was positive and hopeful. She could do a Rubik's Cube in under a minute, and she could look at almost any maths problem and solve it immediately. Her autism was so mild, I hardly noticed it. I liked her right away.

Many people still talk about the episode on *Love Is Mental* where Ben met Robyn. I get it. I really do. It was a funny date, and clearly they both liked each other. It was the show's season two Peter-and-Stefanie moment. They met in a restaurant and right away they started talking about football. Through some weird coincidence, Robyn was an Arsenal fan too. It was the perfect icebreaker and they went on to talk about gaming and TV shows and favourite movies. Ben also drew a picture for Robyn on a napkin. It was a drawing of one of their favourite Miyazaki characters. Robyn loved it and, had she not sneezed and blown her nose accidentally in the napkin, she would have kept it forever. (So she said.)

'Don't worry,' said Ben. 'But Robyn?'

'Yes, Ben.'

'I would really like to draw another picture for you.'

'Are you asking me out on another date, Ben?'

'Yes,' Ben said nervously.

'I would like that, Ben.'

'You would?'

Ben was over the moon. And, so it seemed, was Robyn. They hugged when they left each other and Ben said, quietly to the cameras when Robyn had gone: 'I would like to kiss her one day. That is my dream.'

5

There was another *Love Is Mental* date where the two of them went to an art museum. They walked around and Ben told Robyn all about the paintings and she nodded enthusiastically. She also had a very sound knowledge of history, so that every time Ben would say something like, 'Constable painted this in 1816' Robyn would point out a number of other historical things that also happened in 1816. They both listened to each other with great intensity, nodding at each other. They really did seem connected and, for a moment, it seemed as if they understood each other perfectly.

At the end of the second *Love Is Mental* date, it was agreed that they liked each other and would go on seeing each other. But Ben still didn't get his kiss (much to the disappointment of the producers). That moment, when saying goodbye, came and went in a flash. Ben was too nervous and unsure. He'd never kissed a girl before, ever.

He said to me a few days later: 'Howie, I need your help.'

'What is it?'

'I want to kiss Robyn, but I don't know how.'

'You put your lips on hers and just keep them there.'

'In the movies they put their tongues inside each other's mouths. It seems very odd to me that they do that.'

'You don't have to kiss her, you know. Don't put pressure on yourself.'

'But is kissing… Do you have to use tongues?'

'No. Lips are fine. There are a lot of ways to kiss. And anyway, think about what Robyn would want.'

'Oh, yes. I never thought about that.'

'I suggest you keep your mouth closed when you kiss her. It will be okay. You should put your mouth on hers, and then just wait to see what she does.'

'Maybe she will want to use her tongue.'

'Maybe.'

'I can do that, if she wants me to.'

'Good. Keep your options open.'

Silence.

'Howie?'

'Yes, Ben?'

'When do you do it? When do you know it's the right time?'

'Ben. Ben. Ben. That is the golden question.'

'Why is it *golden*?'

'It's hard to know.'

'Oh, okay.'

I had to think about this. When is the right time to kiss a woman? I challenge anyone to come up with an easy answer to this. I mean, there is no easy answer. You rely on a hunch, right? I mean, I guess we look for cues. We look for signals. But you never truly know. Not when you're kissing that woman for the first time. You never truly know if she wants you to or not.

'Ben,' I said. 'You ask. That's what you should do. You ask her if it's okay if you kiss her.'

'That's not what they do in the movies, Howie.'

'I know. But we've talked about this before. The movies aren't real, Ben. Real life is different. In real life love is much more complicated.'

'Yes, I guess. And I know now. Because I love Robyn.'

'How do you know?'

'I want to do things for her. I want to make her happy, Howie.'

'That's beautiful, Ben. She is lucky to have you loving her.'

'It's complicated, isn't it, Howie? You know what I mean? I can feel that in my head. It's complicated. When to kiss her. When to tell her I love her.'

'One thing at a time, Ben. Remember, we talked about this. For the moment you can show her you care but you don't have to say anything. Not yet. Okay? Let's reel her in.'

'Like a fish.'

'I suppose so.'

5

'It's nice when you catch a fish.'

So *Love Is Mental* season two finished and then it was just Ben and Robyn (and me and Robyn's mother chaperoning). We all agreed that the best way to go forward would be to schedule weekly dates and see how things progress after a few months. So one day we sat in our kitchen, Robyn and her mum along with Ben and I, and we made a schedule. Everyone sat with a notepad and pen in hand:

'What about Saturdays?' Robyn asked.

'I usually go the Emirates,' said Ben. 'But it depends, sometimes there are away games and sometimes Arsenal play on Sundays.'

'I would like to do that,' said Robyn.

'Oh, that's awkward, we only have two seats and all the other seats are taken.'

'Maybe we can fix that,' I said. 'For example, if Chapstick doesn't want to go to a match. We could give Robyn Chapstick's seat.'

'That's a good idea,' said Ben.

'Well, Robyn dear,' said Robyn's mother, 'you don't like big crowds, remember?'

'That's true.'

'Oh,' said Ben. 'Then let's forget that.'

'Why don't we leave that one for now?' I said. 'That might be something for the future. I suggest you look at Fridays.'

'Friday is our game day, Howie.'

'Sure, but…'

'I go swimming on Friday at the pool,' said Robyn.

'Oh, that's nice,' said Ben.

The thing was, both of them had full schedules for the whole week. Of course they did. This was how they both coped with life, having daily routines, having simple daily expectations that were relatively easy to fulfil. At first neither of them seemed to want to budge, to fit each other into their schedules, but finally, with prompting from Robyn's mother and myself, they both agreed that they would meet on Monday afternoons, under Robyn's mother's supervision, and Friday afternoons, under my supervision. It was agreed. When Robyn and her mother left, Ben insisted on writing out the new schedule in full. He put a small heart next to Robyn's name, as he entered her into the schedule. I looked at him and began to worry. A new schedule. What if it all fell apart? He would have to write out the whole schedule again.

But the dating went well and, as the football season ended, Ben was happy to adjust the schedule to fit Robyn in on weekends. He also fit into her schedule a bit, going swimming with her and taking walks. Eventually, it wasn't necessary for me or Robyn's mother to be there all the time. They seemed to understand each other, and they seemed to have a calming effect on each other and they felt stronger together. It was lovely to see.

Eventually Ben came home, from a walk in the park, and he said that he kissed Robyn. 'She used her tongue,' he said.

'Really?'

'She said she had a boyfriend before. They practised kissing a lot.'

'Okay, did you like it?'

'Yes. We had mints before we started. She said that was the best way. It was nice, Howie. Strange, but nice. She said I was good at it.'

I couldn't help but be envious. Robyn was beautiful, kind, and she had no trace of deceit or cynicism about her. She was sweet in every way. I understood Ben's enthusiasm. She was wonderful. And, well, here is where I have to start getting frank, and start fessing up. Because, the ugly truth was that Robyn was becoming more and more attractive to me, every time I saw her. I was becoming confused. I came to the conclusion that Robyn, like Ben, really bore the essence of what I would call a 'beautiful soul'. I was happy for Ben. I truly was. But, unfortunately, I was also jealous.

Yes, you heard correctly. I was jealous of the love my brother had found. It's pathetic, I know, but there it is. The love that seemed to be building between them seemed pure to me. It looked like true love. Truer love, it seemed, than anything I had ever known. And maybe that was the truth. Maybe I had never really been in love before and maybe my romantic history was nothing but an illusion. Was I kidding myself? What did I know about love? And every question Ben would ask me, about love and about what he should do next – every time he asked, I realized I knew less and less. He was asking the wrong person. *He* knew more about love than me. He understood love better than me. He was living proof, in fact, that love existed.

Everything was turning around. Upside down. Backwards. I had to stop pretending. It occurred to me that the authority in my relationship to my brother was based on a flimsy platform of well-rehearsed pretence. It was all a lie. It was all pretend. And this farce only worked because both Ben and I bought in to the lie. He listened because he believed I knew better. I talked, because I also believed I knew better. But I know now. One big fat lie. I had so much to learn from my brother. And as I looked at him with Robyn, I came to realize that I desperately wanted to have what he had. I wanted to feel that love. I wanted to feel it the way he felt it.

* * *

Around this time, Chapstick, Pontiac and I were having one of our roundtable discussions at the pub. Ben was there, and Robyn too. They were playing, and winning, checkers against Bea and Topper. It was after a win at the Emirates so I was feeling quite good about everything.

'So,' said Chapstick. 'Name three must-have songs that you would have on any playlist for someone you've just started dating.'

'I am not sure this can be done,' said Pontiac. 'I mean, it depends on the woman. Right? For example, if she has brown eyes…'

'"Brown Eyed Girl",' I said.

'Exactly.'

'C'mon,' said Chapstick. 'You know there are staples. I grant you, that there are variations, perhaps thematically and depending on what you have deciphered from the woman's taste. But we all know, there are songs that are instant choices.'

'Should they be suggestive?' I asked.

'"Let's Get it On",' Pontiac said and we laughed.

'That's actually pretty good,' said Chapstick, and he wrote it down on a piece of paper.

'You're taking notes?' I said.

'I'll tell you why soon,' said Chapstick.

'"Are You The One That I've Been Waiting For",' said Pontiac.

Chapstick also wrote this down. 'That's good man. You're on a roll.'

'"I Want to Hold your Hand",' I said and we all laughed.

Chapstick didn't write that one down.

'Miles?'

'Too specific and heavy,' said Pontiac. 'You have to have words.'

'Yes,' said Chapstick. 'I think you can go moderately popular. Not too pop. Not too obscure.'

'"When the Party's Over" by Billie Eilish,' I said.

'Not bad. Not too obvious. Very popular though. I'll stick that in the *maybe* column. But I like the idea of songs by women.'

'It's hard to beat "River" by Joni Mitchell,' I said.

Everyone agreed and Chapstick wrote that one down.

The conversation went on like this for a while and here's how it panned out:

Pontiac's three choices: 'Is This Love', 'Let's Get it On'

and 'Fix You' (a left field choice, we thought, but a sure thing according to Pontiac, even if Coldplay had become somewhat unfashionable of late).

Chapstick's three choices: 'I Want You', 'Amelia' (this will explain itself soon) and 'Warm Love'.

And then mine: 'River', 'Fall at Your Feet', 'Jamaica Say You Will'.

But, if you asked me half an hour later, I would have chosen three other songs, probably. It was an impossible task. We all came to the conclusion that Pontiac was right to begin with: there are no sure-fire songs for a playlist. You just have to do it on gut instinct.

When Pontiac left, both Chapstick and I agreed to have one more beer. It was getting late, and I knew Ben would be getting tired soon (Robyn had already been picked up by her mum) but both of us agreed that we needed to talk to each other.

Chapstick came back with two pints and we were about to talk at the same time when Chapstick said, 'You go first.'

'Well,' I said. 'It's not really important or anything. I was just wondering if you've watched *Love Is Mental*?'

'Sure, when is Ben's season coming out?'

'Early autumn.'

'It sure has changed his life, hasn't it?'

'I am going to be honest, Chapstick. I find the show rather upsetting.'

'Why? It's the perfect show to get the word out about autism. And look at Ben. He's really happy. And Robyn's a gem.'

'Well, that's just it.'

'What?'

'Do you find any of the women on the show attractive?'

'Attractive? Um, what are you getting at? I mean, if I say no, then you could accuse me of being prejudiced or something? If I say yes, you're probably going to think I'm a weirdo, or someone wanting to take advantage of those less advantaged than me.'

'No,' I said, hesitating. 'I don't know. I don't mean what you think I mean, I think. I just... It upsets me. These people are the sweetest, kindest, most loving people you would ever want to meet. It's almost as if, if you take everything negative away from the so-called *normals* out there, what you get is a person with autism.'

'Yeah, I can see that. I see what you're getting at. Yes, in that way, they are very attractive. If that's what you mean... Strange choice of words though.'

I sank my mouth into my beer and took three very large gulps. For a moment our minds were distracted, as there were highlights on the TV of Arsenal's victory that day. As each goal hit the net, both Chapstick and I quietly cheered.

'What did you want to tell me then?' I asked him, desperately wanting to leave the subject I just brought up.

'Well,' he said, a sheepish smile coming to his face. 'That's why I was asking you guys about the playlist. I met this woman at work, Amelia, who I have started to date. We've only been on three dates. I am going to make her a playlist.'

'You're making her a playlist? Already? So it's serious then?'

He nodded.

I looked vaguely away. I glanced again at the TV, hoping against hope that the highlights of the game would be shown again. My face was blank, perhaps drawn.

'What's up?' asked Chapstick.

'Nothing. Nothing. I am happy for you.'

'No, you're not.'

'I am.'

'It was bound to happen one of these days.'

'I thought we agreed that we were done with women?'

Chapstick laughed at that, but I looked at him quite seriously.

'Oh c'mon!' he said. 'We're never done with women, and they are never done with us. It's a thing that never gets done.

You know that.'

'You said…'

'They were words. Words bred out of hurt.'

'How do you know you won't get hurt again?'

'I don't. All I know is that it's time to try again. I felt something the moment I saw her. She's beautiful. To me anyway.'

'So it was love at first sight?' I said sarcastically.

'Look,' Chapstick said. 'You're my best friend, you know. It's always going to be that way. We're still going to have our record nights. Though I wouldn't mind changing the schedule on that…'

'She's getting in the way already.'

'Don't be a dick. And the football; you don't think I'll ever give up on the Arsenal?'

'Is she a gooner?'

'She's actually a Geordie.'

'Are you joking?'

'No. But she doesn't really like football much. But she thinks it's funny that I do. She told me that secretly, back in the day, she always thought Thierry Henry was hot.'

'Well she's got taste, I suppose.'

I knew what I had to do. I had to accept this. My best friend was dating and I knew that adjustments would have to be made. First my brother finds love, and now my best friend. It felt like the world was tumbling down a little.

I raised my glass and said, 'Let's drink to it. Let's drink to Amelia.'

'I knew you'd come around,' he said, a huge grin on his face.

I smiled back at him.

When I got home that night, I got Ben in bed and then I watched an episode of *Love Is Mental* from season one. It was the one where Peter first met Stefanie. And I started crying. Bawling, in fact.

Ben came out and said, 'Are you okay, Howie?'

I tried wiping the tears off my face and I looked at him with a forced smile. He went to the refrigerator and he came over to me with a mint wafer. 'Here you go, Howie,' he said. 'This usually makes me feel better.' He handed me the wafer and then he went back to bed. 'Goodnight, Howie.'

'Goodnight, Ben.'

* * *

I'm not proud of what happened next. And I'd like to say my bad behaviour stopped there, but it didn't. It's all a bundle of shit really. But it happened. And nothing can change that. So here goes...

It was a Friday afternoon. It was still off-season. Chapstick, as he was wont to do in those days, had blown me off regarding our listening session that night. So, impromptu and all, we decided that we were going to cook spaghetti for Robyn. Ben would do the spaghetti, and I would make a sauce. 'A good plan,' I told him.

As usual, Robyn and Ben had been gaming all afternoon, taking turns on a dystopian, story-based game called *The Last of Us*. They were both so embroiled in the game that I had to get them off it and suggest that we start preparing for dinner.

Robyn was allowed one glass of wine so I let her open a bottle. Ben watched her curiously, struggling with the bottle between her legs and wiggling the corkscrew wildly. Ben asked her if he could help but then, suddenly, the cork popped. Robyn asked Ben if he wanted a glass but he just shook his head. 'I don't like alcohol,' he said solemnly, looking at the bottle suspiciously.

We ate around the table, something that rarely happened in our apartment. They talked about the game they'd been playing obsessively. I asked Robyn if she liked her new job. (She had just been hired as mail-sorter at a big legal firm.)

'I really like it actually. They said I could come up with a new system.'

'Colour coding?' asked Ben. 'That's what I would do. I would colour code.'

'I haven't decided yet,' said Robyn. 'It's a big responsibility and I want to get it right.'

She seemed to get a bit ditsy and as she drank her one glass I drank the rest of the bottle. I was getting a little tipsy myself. We had a dessert, Ben's favourite: pre-packaged chocolate mousse. After having one, they both asked if they could have another. They ended up eating three each, and laughing because they wouldn't usually be allowed to eat three.

As the night wore on, I started thinking about how pretty Robyn was. How beautifully innocent she looked and how cool she was as she delicately drummed her fingers on the table. She had a way of declaring things, and then leaning back and smiling. I couldn't help but laugh along with her every whim.

'You should be a comedian,' I told her.

'Do you think I'm funny?' she said, looking at me seriously.

'In a good way,' I said.

'Is there a bad way?' she asked.

I guess I didn't want to get into the nuances of the word 'funny' so instead I looked at her hand and I saw that she was wearing a small sapphire ring. 'I like your ring,' I said.

'It's a sapphire,' she said. 'It's my birth stone.'

I nodded.

'Do you know how long it takes for a flight to the moon?' she asked.

I was delighted to talk about space. 'About three days,' I said.

'I was going to say seventy-three hours,' she said, looking at me impressed.

At about this time Ben went off to the loo. And I remember, at that particular moment, feeling suddenly drunk. It was odd, at that moment when Ben left. It was like some kind of mental interference, static in my head, had also left the room. There was this kind of grainy space-like silence. I remember looking at Robyn and a penny dropped. I was very attracted to this woman. And I asked myself: what's wrong with that? Why not? She's beautiful. She deserves to be told so.

So I said, 'You're very pretty, you know.'

She laughed. 'I like your eyes,' she said. 'They remind me of Bradley Cooper.'

'Oh,' I said, and we just went on looking at each other.

We kissed. Yes. We did that.

Did I kiss her? Did she kiss me? I guess, if I am honest, I probably kissed her. And what surprised me, really astonished me actually, is that she could really kiss. Ben was right. She was good at it.

She laughed after the kiss and looked at me and laughed again.

'You really know how to kiss, Robyn,' I said.

'I had a boyfriend,' she said matter-of-factly. 'We used to kiss all the time. We read stuff online about how to do it and stuff. I think we got pretty good at it.'

'You did,' I said.

And then Ben came back to the table and the grainy silence turned into an awkward silence. Ben looked at both of us and wondered why everything had suddenly gone quiet. Nobody knew what to say. Until...

Robyn said, 'Awkward!'

Ben smiled and said, 'What?'

'He kissed me,' Robyn said and she pointed at me, the accused.

'Okay,' Ben said, and he looked at me, and then he looked down at the table.

'He's a good kisser actually,' Robyn said, again, in that matter-of-fact way.

'Okay,' Ben said, and he wouldn't look at me. He just looked at the empty mousse cartons. 'I think you should go now,

Robyn,' he said.

She simply nodded, got up and called her mother.

'Ben…' I said.

He goggle-fingered me, and then he shouted: 'The truth! You can't handle the truth!'

There was more shouting when Robyn's mother found out what had happened. She stood at my door and let me know, in no uncertain terms, how sick I was. She called me exploitative. She accused me of #me-too-ing her daughter, which, to be honest, I thought was a bit harsh and technically not correct. But I took it all in. I looked at her, at her face of rage, and I just listened as she swore and told me what a bad fucking human being I was. Behind her stood Robyn, playing a game on her phone. While the tirade was being blasted at me, Robyn simply looked up from her game and smiled at me. It wasn't sinister. It was the smile of someone engaged in something else. It was the smile of someone who had already moved on. Meanwhile, I was still thinking about what an awesome kisser she was. Her mother was right, of course, to lambast me. Her mother slammed my own door in my face. And all I could hear from Ben's bedroom was: 'The truth! You can't handle the truth!'

I never saw Robyn again. And, of course, Ben never saw her again either. I had broken up my brother's only ever meaningful relationship with the opposite sex. I killed a little of his hopes that day. The experiment with *Love Is Mental* had become a failure. Not because of untoward luck or fate, or divine intervention. But just because of me. What a fuckwit. What a knob. What a piece of steaming doo-doo. Woeful, all of it, to say the least.

6

I went to work as usual on Monday. As said before, my work involves taking care of young kids with autism. When I say taking care of them, I mean babysitting really. I sit in a large playroom and watch over the kids while they are playing, or drawing, or reading. Sometimes they ask me to join in and I will play a game of cards, or Monopoly, or help them build something with Lego. But, for the most part, I leave them to do what they want. Often, they are in between appointments with therapists, or doctors, so keeping them calm is my remit. And I enjoy it. I have got to know the kids over time, and they have got to know me. Little Timmy has an interest in trains and trainspotting and he shows me pictures of trains and he shows me their numbers in his 'train book' and how many times he has registered a look at each train. Jenny B can be difficult. She loves her computer games and her Gameboy, which aren't allowed in the Centre's rec area. So I try and set her up with a puzzle or a quiz book. She can be impatient at first, but when I explain the similarities between some of the challenges presented in the books and her computer games, she usually gets it, and she gets into the task more readily. Leela is five and she doesn't talk. Not a word. She comes and sits beside me and she holds my hand. I don't look at her much, as I can tell she doesn't like that, but I stay close, until finally I offer her a beanbag in front of the TV. And Mickey, Mickey is a little wonder. He claps his hands and whistles and he can tell the pitch of any noise he hears. 'C sharp, Howie! C sharp!' There are many others too. All wonderful kids. And I mean that. Sometimes people who take care of or teach young kids suggest there are always a few bad apples that cause problems (meaning extra work for the carer or teacher) but I've never seen that in the eight years or so of working at the Centre.

I realize I might be painting an idealized view of autism

here. I shouldn't. It's not ideal. Not for the people who have it. It *is* a disability. And for some it's completely debilitating. But a lot of their problems stem from the way society labels them. In fact, labelling them 'disabled' is merely a societal mechanism – a way for society to cope. Society needs to distinguish, and is hardwired to discriminate. So, I know autism is not an ideal thing and it's not a super power, okay? All I am saying is that I have never ever had *real* problems with an autistic kid. But I also understand that largely I work in an environment where autism is understood and accepted as being normal. We take care of it. If a kid goes into a fit or a tantrum or they close themselves off by hiding in a corner, we've got ways to deal with that. So of course this shit happens. They are human. They freak out, like all humans do. And because they can't communicate well, they might seem to freak out in a much bigger way, because they just can't get their point across. That's when you sit down and you try to calm them, and you look at them, and you tell them you're trying to understand. And that's what you do – you try and understand. And when you try, you pretty much always get some kind of an answer. And when the answer comes, in whatever form, they calm down and they forgive, and they love, and they want to engage. Because that's all they need, really, is to be understood. The rest of life follows that. If you can be understood, surely you can be loved. And if you can understand, you can love. Isn't this so? So, what I mean is that I love these kids. I don't pressure them with love. I just sit back and observe, try to understand, and love them for who they are. I think, even if I do say so myself, I am pretty good at my job.

Well, Marsha thinks so too. So, it was with some regret that she pulled me out of the rec-room that Monday morning and asked me to her office. She sat me opposite her, her desk between us, and she considered me with weary eyes, which peaked out over her thin-rimmed glasses.

'Do you know why you are here?' she asked.

'Is it something to do with Robyn Smith?'

'Yes.'

'I suppose her mother called. She was very angry on Friday.'

'She was very angry today.'

I had already decided in advance to lie about this situation. Again, I'm not proud of this. But I didn't want to lose my job and I didn't want anyone, especially someone like Marsha, to think that I am exploitative or a #me-too-er of autistic women.

'She said you kissed Robyn.'

'Robyn said I kissed her?'

'Is it true?'

'No.'

'So Robyn is lying?'

'I don't think she is lying.'

'Howie...'

'I mean, I think she thinks I kissed her. She said she liked my eyes. She said they were like Bradley Cooper's.'

'Your eyes are nothing like Bradley Cooper's.'

I was a little taken aback by this. I had looked at my eyes quite a bit over the weekend and while it took me a bit, I did eventually come to see a resemblance to Bradley Cooper.

'I don't know Robyn to be a liar,' Marsha continued. 'But she is prone to fantasy at times. She's a rom-com buff.'

'I think she liked me and she projected. It was all quite harmless.'

'And then she thought that you kissed her?'

'Yes. And then she told Ben that, which has caused all sorts of problems, as you can understand. They were seeing each other.'

'I know. I actually talked to Ben this morning. He said he didn't see the kiss.'

'You've known me for many years, Marsha. You know I wouldn't do that.'

'You're a very good carer, Howie. You have a real instinct with the kids. Sometimes I wish you'd studied and got some qualifications so I could have you here working with them all the time.'

'Thank you. So you're not going to fire me?'

'You have to be careful, Howie. Not just for the Centre's sake, but also for your own sake and especially your brother's sake. To be honest, Robyn doesn't seem one bit bothered by any of this. It's her mother that's freaked out.'

'I understand. I don't blame her mother. She's just looking out for her kid.'

'Well, if she's down here, just keep out of her way. I guess Ben and Robyn won't be seeing each other anymore?'

'Ben feels hurt. Disappointed. But I'm sure it will be okay. I will talk to him.'

* * *

It was Thursday, later that week, when Ben and I took a day trip out to the countryside. We took a train out to a nature reserve on the outskirts of the city. The train took an hour and a half to get there, and, well, if it's not too intolerable, I'd like to mention an incident on the train.

You see, I've already explained the hostile approach to autism. How some people see 'stupidity' and react aggressively. But there's also the other side. How some people see 'stupidity' but act with well-intentioned condescension.

A middle-aged woman, who introduced herself as Marjorie, was sitting across the aisle from us. She had got wind of the fact that Ben had autism, and she said that she had a good understanding of autism because her grandchild was autistic.

'Okay,' I said.

So she leaned over and talked to Ben as if he was five years old, and deaf.

'So, Ben, do you like trains?'

'Not really,' said Ben.

'Ben's thirty-five,' I stated.

'Look,' said Majorie. 'I've got some chewing gum. Do you want a piece of chewing gum, Ben?'

'You're so kind,' I said. 'But do you mind just keeping a little distance there, between you and Ben?'

I could see Ben getting tense.

Sometimes I wonder if it's me. Does he pick up on my signals? Is he picking up on my impatience, and where that might lead? In any case, he started ringing his hands. I reminded Marjorie, for the second time, to keep her voice down, but she just wouldn't, or couldn't. I tried to give her the benefit of the doubt. I knew she was well intentioned. I knew that she wanted to be nice. Eventually she got off the train and both Ben and I were instantly relieved. Not just relieved about her leaving, but relieved that I wasn't pushed to asking her to shut the fuck up. It has happened before. And I can't tell you how bad I feel afterwards. It's easy to tell some fuckwad, who is being aggressive towards Ben, to fuck off. But telling a well-meaner, who is just plain ignorant of what it means to have autism, to fuck off, well, it never feels good after the act. These things always come out the wrong way and it's always down to my impatience. I just hate anyone condescending to my brother. Like I said before. He's not stupid. He's just different.

The nature reserve was beautiful. There was an easy-going hiking track, winding in and out of wooded areas, and ponds with water lilies and ducks. Ben had a pair of binoculars and a book and was trying to spot the birds. It wasn't something he'd done before. He saw it as a puzzle. And once he got the hang of the book, he was able to identify goldfinches, great and coal tits, robins and we even saw a lovely little jay. 'I think the jay is my favourite, Howie,' he told me.

We walked up a small rise and we found a bench where we decided to have lunch. We had peanut butter sandwiches and chocolate milk for lunch.

6

'You know, Ben, I've been meaning to talk to you about Robyn,' I said, my eyes focused on some tiny ducklings swimming furiously behind their mother on a pond.

'It's okay, Howie,' Ben said, chewing on his sandwich. 'You don't need to. I love you, Howie.'

'I know, Ben. And I love you too. But let's just have one talk about this, okay?'

'Okay, Howie.'

'Well how do you feel about it?'

'Robyn was fun. But I guess she wasn't the right one, Howie.'

'But you miss her?'

'No. It was disappointing at first. And then it was inconvenient having to redo the schedule. But now I don't think about her at all.'

'Okay.'

'But I think life is really good, Howie. I like it when it's just you and me. There aren't any problems when it's just you and me. We don't need complications, do we, Howie?'

'But don't you still want to fall in love?'

'No.'

'But why?'

'It's disappointing, Howie.'

'Well, we talked about that. It's not supposed to be easy.'

'It's okay, Howie.'

'I want that for you, Ben. I want you to love someone. I am so sorry I fucked that up for you, Ben. I am sorry.'

'It's okay, Howie. It really is. You know what they say: it takes two to tango.'

'Do you know what that means?'

'Of course, silly. It means that it wasn't just your fault, Howie. It's okay. I understand that Robyn liked you and not me.'

'I think she liked you.'

'A fine mess.'

'A fine mess.'

'You can fall in love, Howie. I won't stop you from falling in love.'

'Maybe I am done with women.'

'You want to fall in love, Howie.'

'No.'

'Yes.'

'Okay, let's just leave it at that.'

'Yes. Let's just leave it at that, Howie.'

We walked around the reserve for another hour and then back to the train station. We were both quite tired and we didn't talk on the way home on the train. But Ben held my hand. I looked out of the train and began to wonder where my life was going. What was I doing? Was Carrie right when she said I had no direction, that I had no ambition? What was the point of it all? I wondered, too, if Ben was right. Did I want to fall in love again?

* * *

Since the Robyn incident, I was pretty much taking Ben everywhere with me, except work. I guess I was trying to make it up to him. I guess, deep down, I knew I would never be able to make it up to him. But he seemed happy to tag along and I knew, if I kept him close, he would be okay. I guess it was all about guilt and what a fucking terrible human being I am. But anyway...

It was a Wednesday evening and Chapstick, Ben and I were doing the rounds at the record shops. It was the first time Chapstick and I had even seen each other in two weeks. Apparently things with his new girlfriend, Amelia, were going just grand. I must admit, I was feeling prickly that day. I couldn't help it. I was a bit resentful that Chapstick was choosing his girlfriend over me.

'It's not like that,' he said, as he scoured through a box of second-hand albums. He pulled out an old Dean Martin record, *Dean Martin Sings*, and looked it over.

'I prefer later Deano,' I said.

'It's a bit pastiche and banal though, don't you think?'

'Oh yes,' I said. 'But deliberately so.'

We both agreed. Banality was certainly not off the cards for us. Recently we'd both taken a liking to the fad *lounge music*.

'Anyway, as I said, it's not like that with me and Amelia,' Chapstick said. 'It's not as though she is taking over any part of my life. We are just incorporating each other.'

'Syncing schedules,' said Ben, who was also looking in the boxes.

'Exactly,' said Chapstick. 'And it's early days, Howie. You know how it is in the beginning of a relationship.'

'Sex all the time.'

'There's that. But there's also just being together and exploring our likes and dislikes. You know? I am meeting her friends and stuff.'

'Oh great. New friends.' I said this as if it was the worst thing in the world.

'Take it easy, Howie. Amelia wants to meet you too.'

'And me?' asked Ben.

'Of course, Benny boy. You too.'

'Well, it's about time,' I said.

'In fact, Amelia has this friend, Rita.'

'Rita?'

'She is single. We could double date.'

'A blind date?'

Chapstick laughed. 'Yeah, why not?'

'Let me think about it,' I said.

At that moment Ben pulled out *The Good Son* by Nick Cave. 'You like Nick Cave, don't you, Howie?'

'Mate, that's his best album and, for reasons inexplicable, I don't have it. Good on ya, Ben!'

I took it from him and he beamed a proud smile at me.

'It's not you know,' said Chapstick.

'What?' I said.

'It's not his best album.'

'Of course it is. It's a fact. A well-known fact.'

'*The Boatman's Call*. You even said so yourself – that it's the best breakup album ever.'

'Which is why I can't possibly listen to it, ever.'

'It's not the best breakup album either. *Blood on the Tracks*.'

'We already agreed to disagree on that one.'

'*The Boatman's Call* is still Cave's best record. You know it. I know it. The world knows it. It's a fact.'

'Oh fuck off, Chapstick!' I said abruptly and this outburst surprised all three of us. Chapstick and I, as long as we've known each other, have rarely raised our voices to each other. We disagree about some things. Not a lot, but some. But if we come to the end of a discussion without a resolution we just shrug it off, with that kind of friendly assurance that we agree to 99% of everything else. So, it was a bit surprising that I snapped at him.

'Sorry about that, Chapstick,' I said softly.

'That's okay, Howie. After all, it all comes down to taste, you know?'

'Yeah, you're right.'

I bought *The Good Son* and Chapstick bought Joni Mitchell's *Blue* and Billie Eilish's *When We All Fall Asleep, Where Do We Go?* because he was sure Amelia would like them. And we bought Ben a record, because he liked the cover: The Small Faces' *Ogdens' Nut Gone Flake*. Well, we had this record on heavy rotation and, as you can imagine (if you're familiar with the record), it sparked Ben into drawing the most fantastic images and making up new nonsensical phrases:

'Humpty dumpty eats the moonfood; all gobbly gobbly without a shell' and 'and they altogether lived spankily spankily whack-a-doodle ever after'.

'You're absolutely mad,' I told him, when he started muttering these things to himself.

'Happiness Stan is mad, isn't he, Howie?'

'Mad as a hatter,' I said and this made Ben laugh hysterically.

Anyway, I digress, again. So, back on track, it turns out that Robyn had told Ben about *Ogdens' Nut Gone Flake* and, when he mentioned this on our way out of the shop, Chapstick asked:

'So what happened to Robyn, Ben?'

'Howie kissed her.'

'He did what?' Chapstick swung around and looked at me.

'Well...' I muttered.

'It's okay,' said Ben.

'No,' said Chapstick firmly. 'It's not okay, Ben. Howie isn't allowed to kiss your girlfriend.'

'Robyn and I talked on the phone,' said Ben. 'And she said maybe we could be just friends.'

'Is that what you want?'

'It's okay.'

'You still like her?'

'No. She wasn't the right fish, Chapstick.'

Chapstick shook his head and we exited the shop.

We walked a bit in silence. The traffic was busy. People were coming home from work. It looked like it might rain. But it didn't.

Chapstick then said: 'Well, you should know, Howie, Carrie invited me to her wedding.'

'What?' I said, quite taken aback.

'I think she thinks I'm still with Melinda. Is that possible?'

'Is Melinda going?'

'I think so.'

'Yeah that would be awkward.'

'No, not really. I'll be taking Amelia.'

'You're actually *going*?'

'Yeah, why not? I like Carrie. I always liked her.'

'Well, I'm not going,' I said defiantly.

'Yeah, and you're not invited. She told me that over the phone. She said your breakup was pretty harsh on you, and that she thought you might make a scene.'

'For fuck's sake! It's been eight years or something. I was with Bridget after that. You can tell her that Bridget was the one that hurt me the most. Not her. Not Carrie.'

'Well don't get weird about it.'

'You think I'm getting weird about it? Chapstick, you're going to my ex's wedding. Isn't that weird?'

'No. She said that she, Melinda and I were really good friends back in the day. And she really felt good about us coming.'

'Not weird? As if I don't even know her? I lived with her Chapstick! I saw her dirty undies every day. I smelled her farts.'

'You can't handle the truth!' Ben suddenly declared.

'You're winding Ben up,' said Chapstick.

'She vomited in my suitcase when we were on holiday! I can tell you the noise she used to make when she had orgasms!' I then proceeded to make a noise resembling a cat being squeezed to death.

'You're upsetting Ben, Howie.'

'It's okay,' said Ben.

'And you think,' I continued, 'that it's not weird that you, a person that only came into her life because of me, are going to her wedding, when I, me, the person she lived with, the person she shared everything with for six years, the person she said she loved, isn't going? That's right Chapstick, she loved me. So, me? No. No. No. I'm not invited to the most important day of her life. Yes, this all makes perfect sense. Doesn't it? Doesn't it just?'

After this rant there was a bit of silence as we crossed a road. I held Ben's hand as we crossed and he squeezed it to let me know that everything was going to be okay.

After a little while Chapstick said, 'I won't go to the wedding if you don't want me to.'

I then took a deep breath and shook my head. 'Of course you should go. For fuck's sake, I am just trying to process. It feels like the world just keeps going but I've been left behind at some isolated bus stop in the middle of nowhere.'

'Maybe it's time you listened to *The Boatman's Call* again. It might give you some understanding or some perspective.'

We were poised to go our separate ways. I hugged Chapstick and, now feeling a lot calmer, I said, 'Say hi from me. Send her my regards and let her know that I wish her the best. And say hi to Melinda too. I miss her.'

'You see how it works?'

I nodded.

Ben and I went down to the underground to make our two-stop journey home.

* * *

But the whole Carrie thing ('Carrie-marry-gate' I called it in my head) stuck with me while I cooked dinner, while we watched episode four, season three of *Stranger Things* for the eleventh time, and later, while I got Ben off to bed. I couldn't help it. The three of them, Anna, fucking Carrie and Bridget. They started orbiting me like hovering moons. And I got to wondering if they would always be there, or if one day they would spin out of orbit and get lost in deep space. Or a black hole would hoover them up. Okay, I am not that dumb to believe that a black hole is going to suck up one of my moons, and not suck me up. But maybe that would be okay too. (It's impossible to imagine what happens when you get sucked into a black hole. Am I right? I suppose you're reduced to atoms instantly. I suppose there is nothing left. No you, just residual you, that eventually goes into the making of something else. But I am waffling and digressing again. Blah blah blah. This brain never stops, never lets up and never fails to remind me that I am one fucked up individual.)

And then I did something spontaneous. I started thinking about Anna and wondering desperately what she could be doing. What happened to you, beautiful Anna?

I wondered if her breasts were still enormous or if she still liked sex as much as before. (Probably not, I concluded. No one could survive for long liking it that much.) I wondered if she still had that porcelain face and that irresistible smile. I wondered if she ever thought of me. I wondered if she thought of me fondly. Or missed me. Or would really love to see me. Or maybe she'd like to go out with me again and see if there was still a flame? Maybe she'd want to have sex with me?

'Of course I'm single,' I hear an imagined Anna saying to me. 'Of course I want to have sex with you!' And then we meet and she looks exactly as she did when we were eighteen and we laugh so much and we remember our past fondly and we make love. Only, it's adult love now. We look into each other's eyes. We're better lovers. We're really good at *doing it*.

No, this did not really compute. Everything I knew about sex was from her. All those tricks. She was the one who taught me. I could imagine her saying: 'You're still doing that?' with a distinct look of disappointment on her face.

The more sensible questions hit me: Was she still a nurse? Did she have children? Did she stay with that fuckwad she left me for?

I decided to see if I could find her online, but searching for an Anna Jones proved to be fruitless. There are many Anna Joneses in this world. So many. I gave up on that idea and then I fished out an old journal of mine, a journal that was in a box at the back of my cupboard (where I keep memorabilia, writing, drawings, photos etc.). And in no time at all I found an old phone number to her parents' house.

Anna's mother always liked me, so I was tempted. I could just ask after her, right? But it was getting late. And yet, at the same time, I couldn't let it go. I knew that if I didn't make the call right away, I wouldn't sleep that night. I would just lie in bed, in the dark, thinking about Anna. I had to know. I had to have answers. And I had to have them now. So I dialled the number:

'Hello.'

'Hello, is this Mrs Jones?'

'Yes it is.'

'This is Howie.'

'Howie?'

'Anna's first boyfriend, remember?'

'Oh Howie. Yes. I remember. I think you were her second boyfriend.'

'No. I was her first.'

'No, I think you were her second.'

'Okay, well, how are you?'

'I'm fine thanks. But why are you calling me, Howie? And at this time?'

'Oh I'm sorry. I just haven't been in touch with Anna for some time.'

'Oh.'

'I just wanted to hear how she is, and perhaps, if there is a way, and if she wants to, I thought it could be fun to meet her again.'

'Oh, Howie.'

'Yes?'

There was a long pause then. And I knew it didn't bode well. Telephone conversations are weird like that. Unlike a face-to-face conversation, there is so little to work with. The theatrics all come from pauses and audible expressions, noises and such. But this was a long deathly silence. (Just as a by-the-way, Ben has no clue when it comes to things like this. A telephone call to him is all words, so it's always best to be clear, concise and get straight to the point. Don't expect him to understand cues.)

'Anna passed away about four years ago, Howie.'

And now it was my turn to pause. What does one say when one gets such news? After a few unbearable seconds I mumbled, 'I'm sorry to hear that.'

'She had breast cancer. She left behind two children and a husband.'

I looked at the phone. Should I ask? I shouldn't ask. No, definitely not. But *should* I?

I did: 'It wasn't, by any chance, Harry, the guy she left me for?'

'No, Howie.'

'Okay, good.'

I could almost hear her shaking her head. She took a deep breath. 'Well, have a good life, Howie.'

'Again, I am sorry to hear about Anna. She was a lovely...'

'Goodbye, Howie.'

Any momentum I might have had with this compulsion to call my old girlfriends ended with this call. Of course, Carrie was out of the question anyway, and, to be honest, *fuck her*. But Bridget, what about Bridget? No, I couldn't face that. And that telephone call to Anna's mother just proved that it was better to leave things alone. Just move the fuck on. Don't, whatever you do, look back.

I thought about Anna dying and it hurt me, to be honest. I felt like something had been stripped away from me. You know what they say, something inside me just died. I mean, how did it happen? Anna was so young. She had so much to offer. How could someone having so much to offer – so much vitality, so much to give – die, while unworthy fuckers stalked the streets murdering and raping and being general arseholes? It was so fucked up. The order of things. Or the lack of order. None of it made sense. It was downright unfair. Anna should still be alive.

And that was that really, one phone call and I had lost my

chance to remember Anna as a vital, energetic, passionate, driven human being. Now she was relegated. Now she was just dead. Silent. A cold dead star. Dust. Gone forever.

7

The blind double date happened about two weeks later.

It had been a long hot summer, as they say, and London in the heat can be unforgiving. And it had been an odd, rainless summer. Just fuzzy blue skies, the occasional cloud, dusty pavements and fading grass lawns. The high street was strung out with lazy people, drinking coffee, with nowhere to go. Ben and I kept to our usual schedule. Ben was his usual happy-go-lucky self, as long as we kept to the schedule.

It was still off-season, though the Gunners had played a few friendlies and every day I checked the news to see if they were bringing in that new midfielder from Italy they so desperately needed. On the weekends Ben and I were doing daytrips, either into the city, to a museum or the movies, or out to the countryside for a walk.

I felt like things might get better if I just stuck to Ben's schedule. I felt like I could maybe get rid of this growing anxiety in the pit of my stomach if we had our days full and our minds engaged. And it worked for a bit. But then I started to feel bored. I felt like there was something wrong, but I just couldn't figure out what it was. And there was no one to talk to. Chapstick was otherwise occupied, and anyway, we never talked about intangibles anyway, unless it involved music. Some jazz we liked contained the intangible. I remember a conversation we once had about Maria Schneider, who we both really like. But neither of us had come to understand, or pin down, just what her music was about. *The Thompson Fields,* we both agreed, was a modern masterpiece, but what was it exactly?

'It lulls you,' I remember Chapstick saying. 'And then it blasts you with confusing dissonance.'

'Dissonance.' I agreed.

But you see there? You see what I just did? I diverted my

own thinking. I was talking about the empty pit in my stomach and then, with the click of a finger, I am thinking about *The Thompson Fields*. For fuck's sake, this brain never gives up, does it? I mean, if you think about it, nothing is tangible, right? Existence doesn't offer understanding. Existence is jazz. It will do your head in. The only tangible thing we have is distraction. And I tell you what, you better get on board. Make yourself a fucking schedule. Give your song some structure. Because if you don't, you're just plain fucked. That's my conclusion.

Just thinking this shit hurts my brain; so let me get on with things.

Anyway, our schedule was well broken in August, when Ben went on his annual camping trip, organized by the Centre. This year, Ben and about eight other disabled adults, were going up to Scotland, to Loch Ness no less. He would be gone for a week. He was so excited as he packed and as I bundled him off onto the bus. At one point he was 100% sure that he was going to witness the Loch Ness Monster and he asked me relentlessly, on the tube on the way to the Mental Health Centre, if I believed the monster was real or not.

'Probably not,' I said.

'Yes, probably not,' he said.

'But you know, you never can tell, Ben.'

He got very excited by that, and by the end of the conversation it wasn't so much about whether or not the monster existed, but whether he was going to see it or not.

'What percentage chance do you think I have of seeing the monster, Howie?'

'Very, very small.'

'10%, Howie?'

'Try .0000001%, Ben.'

'Okay, Howie. That's not much. But it's still a chance.'

'I guess so, buddy.' I looked at him and he put his head on my shoulder. 'But don't go up there expecting to see the monster,

Ben. It's much better just to expect to have a good time.'

'Marsha is going.'

'Yes. She will take care of you.'

'Will you miss me, Howie?'

'That's 100%, Ben. That's how much I will miss you.'

When I got back to the apartment I did a little cleaning. I looked at the schedule on the refrigerator and smiled to myself. I was a free man for a week. And then I suddenly felt empty. I don't know what it was. I just sat down and didn't know what to do.

I decided to look at porn and I came to this webcam website and I found myself strangely drawn to a cam that had five people in it – five young adults in a hotel room, somewhere in America, I assumed. I checked the time. Yes, it was night for them. Very, very late. And it was odd. They sat about drinking, and talking to the camera. Two young men and three young ladies. At first they were fully clothed and they talked about various topics. Nothing at all of great interest: bad movies, bad TV shows and bad music. And they were drinking wine. White wine. Their point meter – where patrons donate money – was dead, and yet they just stood, looking at the camera, occasionally looking at each other, now and then laughing or giggling, and they talked. I turned the sound down and I just watched them. I don't know why, but I watched them for hours. What were they doing? What was the purpose to all this?

Slowly they began to undress and I found myself very much attracted to one of the women. She was more curvaceous than the other two. When she was fully undressed I discovered also that she was unshaved. I just stared at her, mostly at her face. Her cheeks dimpled when she smiled. I watched her interact with the others, kissing the other women, touching the men. She looked at the camera confidently. But this wasn't a porn star. This was just an ordinary woman. A beautiful, ordinary woman. In my eyes, an extraordinary, ordinary woman. I wondered about her backstory. I wondered where she came from. I wondered how well she knew the other four. I wondered, as she began to perform oral sex on one of the guys, if she really, *really* was complicit in this whole thing. Sure, she smiled and everything. She seemed to be having a good time, but I couldn't help but ask myself, wouldn't she be happier with someone to love? Someone like me? A schedule?

Out of utter boredom I masturbated and by the time I finished, the five young adults in that hotel room seemed to be mostly asleep. It seemed as if someone had forgotten to turn the camera off and they just lay there, naked on the bed, splayed about like the aftermath of a Roman orgy. I watched them for another half an hour or so. I kept thinking to myself, I should get up. I should go out. I should go for a walk or go get a coffee or I could even go see a movie by myself. But I didn't move. I just watched them, in silence. Until the image finally disappeared.

I did miss Ben. I achingly missed Ben.

* * *

So that same night, the night of that memorable little online soiree with the young men and women in that hotel room, was the night of the blind double date. Well, blind for my part, and, I supposed, Rita's. I didn't want to go, to be honest. I thought to myself that I would be happy just to stay at home and drink some beer and listen to some records that I'd picked up that week. But I had to go. Chapstick had insisted and it had all been set up. And it was Saturday, a rare Saturday without Ben. I didn't have any excuses really, not for Chapstick, and not for myself. I had to go.

We met at an Italian restaurant on the high street. It was a pleasant place, and I realized it had been years, probably since I dated Bridget, that I had been in such a nice place. I ordered gnocchi and we drank some delicious wine from Sicily. And, frankly, it was an okay evening, despite a few uncomfortable moments.

So firstly, let me describe Chapstick's girlfriend, Amelia. She was very exotic looking with some kind of brown Asian blood that I never did get around to asking about (and to which I don't really give a shit to be honest). She was beautiful, but by now it might have become apparent, I really do think so, *so* many women are beautiful. I can see beauty in most of them, usually. The beauty of a woman, even if she's not my type, I'm good at picking that up. And Amelia certainly wasn't my type (but I can't explain what that is, either) but I could see she was a beauty and I liked her a lot. I was so happy for Chapstick. He sat so close to her and he smiled a lot. They really did seem to be completely into each other. Amelia was wonderful, normal, ordinary and likeable. And Chapstick was so proud. She told us about her interest in botany. She studied all that stuff in school. 'She can name any flower,' said Chapstick proudly. 'Any you can point at.' She didn't care much for football, and music to her was what she heard on the radio, but Chapstick didn't care. He told me later that he would move his collection down to the basement for this woman, that was how much he liked her.

Rita. Rita was intimidating. It wasn't that she deliberately set out to intimidate me. Not at all. She was nice. But she was also confident, and assured in her opinions, of which she had many, and she wasn't afraid to initiate conversation and take it anywhere really. I started to think she had no boundaries.

I liked her hair. It was black, long and straight, and remarkably shiny and bouncy. She was in her late thirties and she had those tiny wrinkles by her eyes. Not imposing, and only caught occasionally in the candlelight. The pores on her skin were open too, and again the light from the candle on her face had me thinking about craters on the moon's surface. Here I go again. Don't get me wrong. Her skin pores were not craterous at all. But it was warm in the restaurant. And she had to occasionally dab her face because she thought she might be sweating. All this was done with a great ease, with feminine acumen. She seemed to be on top of everything.

Well, I don't know what kind of picture I am painting here, because the simple fact is that Rita was very attractive and I suppose that's where the intimidation came from. I instantly thought that this woman was out of my league. And, as the night wore on, I was surprised that she had any interest in me at all. She was just so much more interesting, so much more vital, so much more together than me. And yet we kept on talking. And I asked her questions and she asked me questions. She asked about Ben, and she said that she admired me, that I was taking care of my brother.

'It must be a burden,' she said.

'Not really. Is love a burden?'

Her eyes lit up. She liked that. I could tell that using the Ben card, which I had used many times before, could be a way in.

But it wasn't all smooth sailing. As said, Rita was a very solid person. She had solid views. And she was assertive. And bold. So when I said that I thought that people with autism weren't so different to everyone else, she was quick to point out that it depended where on the spectrum they were. She also accused me, subtly, of being an idealist. 'It's no use pretending,' she said, 'that everyone is the same in this world, because they are not. It's very much a part of human nature to discriminate, to differentiate, to place oneself in a position of superiority, so to speak. And there's no use in pretending that the less advantaged of us are in the same bracket as us. Does this do them justice, in their own right? Are we just trying to placate them? Do you see what I mean? We can determine differences, but we can also respect them.'

She was smart. She spoke with confidence. And so did Amelia and I could see that Chapstick was becoming quite comfortable in this atmosphere of adult behaviour and he had some very insightful things to say too. I always knew he was smart, to be honest, but as he and I rarely talked of anything outside of football and music, perhaps I didn't know just how smart he was. He was going through a change, and it was working for him. This whole Amelia thing was working for him.

And for me, well, this whole Amelia thing was sinking my fucking world.

Chapstick and I went to the loo at some point. We stood at the urinal and he smiled at me.

'So... Rita...'

'I keep thinking of *Lovely Rita, meter maid*.'

'*Where would I be without you?*'

'I never thought much of that song.'

'Me neither.'

'And people keep insisting *Sgt. Pepper's* is the greatest album ever.'

'It's just a meme. For those that aren't truly discerning.'

'I agree.'

'Hey, worst Beatles song, ever?'

'"Mr. Moonlight"?'

'Good call. I can't stand "Yellow [fucking] Submarine".'

We started laughing, because now we knew the earworm that was that song would be stuck in our heads for the rest of the night.

'Or "Maxwell's Silver [fucking] Hammer".'

'Or "Obla-[fucking]-di-obla-[fucking]-da".'

And as we washed our hands we both agreed that it was a myth that all Beatles songs were great. Many of them were, of course, but there was some real shit in there too.

This conversation lifted my mood immensely. Chapstick was still Chapstick and always would be Chapstick. He was going to be my best mate, forever, for sure. So why did I feel so threatened?

When I got back to the table I took assertive action. I ordered another bottle of wine and I told the group some jokes that I knew and I could see that Rita was starting to think that I was okay. And I started to think that she was so beautiful and I told her that the candlelight was dancing on her face and she liked that. I told her about poets I liked and she liked that a lot and promised me that she would read the last verse of E.E. Cummings' 'Somewhere I Have Never Travelled, Gladly Beyond' and I just marvelled at the thought of poetry, and how I hadn't read a single line since Bridget and I broke up.

As I began to recognize the new Chapstick I started to see the possibility of a new me, and it felt good. Wow! I even told Amelia how lucky Chapstick was to find someone so nice and Chapstick put his hand on my shoulder. It was an odd thing, and I looked at his hand. It occurred to me that the only time he and I touched each other was at the Emirates when Arsenal scored a goal.

It was becoming a good evening and it hadn't finished yet. I'd love to say it went on in that positive vein, that it was all great and that my chest was puffed out and that I had found myself again. But as ever with me, things weren't far from falling off the edge of a cliff. That's just the way it is, right? Like Arsenal losing against a big side. It's a sure thing. Expect anything else and you're just setting yourself up for disappointment. I don't want to sound as if I'm complaining, but I am, aren't I? Sometimes I just wish I could be someone else. If I could be someone else, everything could start from ground zero. Everything could be okay.

* * *

Rita and I got a cab together and, while it wasn't agreed at the beginning of the cab ride, it became apparent by the end that we were going to get out at the same place. Namely, my apartment. We decided a nightcap would be in order. And I think we both wanted sex, or at least I thought so.

It was strange kissing her, because I still had in mind the last woman I had kissed, Robyn, and I couldn't help but compare. Was Robyn a better kisser? Well, to be fair, I'm no great judge. How many women have I kissed in my life? And really, what constitutes a good kiss? Very subjective I would think. Like music. Anyway, I preferred Robyn's kiss, but that might come down to what happened when things started to progress with Rita and me.

So let me digress, just for a second, and go back to the previous Saturday when Chapstick, Pontiac and I had a discussion in the pub about the best, bang-on seduction record. We all agreed that you can't have anything too distracting, not anything that stands out too much, so there was a tendency to lean towards jazz. Though Pontiac talked a lot about Augustus Pablo and a really interesting German band called Halma.

'Good choices,' Chapstick agreed. 'But I'm going with the Train. *A Love Supreme*. It's mystical, you know, and it lets you in and then releases you. It's almost like sex really. In any case, I'm going to say, it's probably best not to have words.'

But I disagreed. 'Chet Baker,' I said. 'I don't know what it is about Chet, but women really like him. I don't know if it's his voice, or his trumpet, but the guy reels them in. And it's not as though those words are over engaging. It's still jazz, you know what I mean? It's still all about the sound. But I don't know, maybe Chet is the closest voice to an orgasm that I've ever heard.'

They both found this hilarious and we laughed about it on and off the whole night. But I was right, wasn't I? Chet fucking Baker.

So, when I got in that night, I went right to the turntable and put *Chet Baker Sings* on, confident it would fulfil all expectations. And it did not disappoint.

'Oh what's this guys name again?' asked Rita.

'Chet Baker,' I said.

'I like this.'

We kissed standing up at first and then we settled on the sofa. We poured a couple of glasses of wine, but we never really drank them. There was too much else going on.

So where, you might ask, did it start to go wrong?

So, I wouldn't say I'm the best lover ever. But I'm not the worst, either. I think back to Anna (poor dead Anna) and how lucky I was to be with someone, at such a young age, who seemed so advanced and willing to do anything. So, I had garnered a confidence back then that still carried me through these situations. I knew I could carry myself, and represent myself well through these situations. But, right away, I could tell that something was up when I started thinking these things, or thinking too much, really. I wasn't thinking, oh, this is great kissing this beautiful woman on my couch and isn't it going to be great to put my penis inside her. And then... No. No. No. I was thinking about dead Anna and about expectations and about things like: 'what if I'm no good? I probably only have one shot at this, with her, and what if I fuck up? What if I come too early? *What if I can't get it up*?' And that was that really. The moment you think that one, well, you're plain fucked. And then anxiety begot anxiety. I rode with these thoughts and I sank, sank into the mire of floppy uselessness.

What made all this worse is that I really, over the last hours, had grown to like Rita. She was good looking, vivacious, and at ease with herself. And she seemed to like me. Why? Fuck knows. Really, fuck knows.

But it wasn't going to work. She was too good looking – too all of those things that I just mentioned. And, as our kissing and making out went on, I became more and more tense. She even asked me if I was okay at some point. I assured her I was fine and I told her she was beautiful and then we started making out again.

I went down on her, thinking that this would hide the fact that my penis was dead flaccid and that it wasn't under any circumstances going to cooperate. I thought if I was confronted with her genitals it would get me going, that it would distract me enough to stop me overthinking. But it wasn't working.

And then I thought about the girl in the hotel room with her friends on the webcam. That's right, I thought about her and then I thought, well, maybe I wasn't able to blow more than one load a day anymore. Those days were maybe behind me. And obviously, I'd blown that one load already that day.

My next plan of action was to see if I could get her to come by using my tongue and that was a pretty good plan, I thought. I'd just finish her off and then tell her, calmly, that she could finish me off next time, and that would somehow all make sense in this strange, late night, let's-fuck-for-the-first-time atmosphere. But I couldn't get her to come and she kept trying to lift my head and then she said, 'I want you inside me.'

Well, it was impossible to hide from that point onwards. And anyway, no one needs any more details. Suffice to say, she did her very best, at the expense of her unconditioned jaw, to make a difference, but it wasn't going to happen. Not in a million years was it going to happen.

She said it was okay and that 'it happens' and that I needn't worry about it. But I was disconsolate and unforgiving of myself. I again told her how beautiful she was.

'It must be the alcohol,' she said kindly. 'I've heard it does that.'

I called her a cab and I kissed her at the door and she said, 'See you later.' But I knew what it all meant. Yes, we would see each other. How could we not, when we were so close to Chapstick and Amelia? But I knew there wasn't going to be another chance to make love to this beautiful woman. I looked out the window as she got into the cab and I wondered what she was thinking as the cab drove through the empty night streets.

7

What a loser. What was wrong with that guy? Alcohol? I doubt it. He just didn't have what it took, that's all. He just wasn't good enough for me.

I put my tracksuit pants on and I switched the TV on. And then an episode of *Love Is Mental* came on, and I was drawn to watch it. I cried again. I really cried. And, aware that Ben was a long way away, and not listening from his bedroom, I cried very, *very* loudly. I sobbed. I went foetal.

It was like that. Intangible. Lost. Without distraction. Without direction. Without erection. Flaccid. What avenues were left for me? Where, from here? Why, from here?

8

It wasn't always this easy with Ben. Like I've been saying, even though I work around people with autism, and have associated with them all my life, I'm really no expert. I know there isn't just one thing you can call autism, and there are many and extreme degrees on the spectrum, and different traits and personalities. In other words they are all diverse, just like all of us are. You see similar patterns here and there, but essentially an experience with one person with autism isn't going to mean you have an understanding of them all. Ben, for the most part, has been my experience and understanding. And he is an individual, and, as I said, it wasn't always easy with him.

He didn't speak until he was seven. And at seven he merely started parroting, either us, his family, or the TV. We came to understand that certain phrases from TV actually had a larger meaning, like the phrase from *The Godfather*: 'Revenge is a dish best served cold.' He'd deliver this in a very strange husky voice, and it usually meant that he was hungry. He also got 'I'm gonna make him an offer he can't refuse,' from *The Godfather*. This meant he wanted to go the park to play on the swings. I know it sounds weird. Another favourite movie of his was *Wayne's World* and he wasn't averse to getting down on his knees and chanting: 'We're not worthy! We're not worthy!' He did this for me often, because I would crack up laughing. Looking back, I think it meant that he loved me. I like to think that.

But there were loads of people that just didn't get Ben. Nearly everyone really. For a while there, it seemed like all of society was conspiring against him. Teachers, doctors, carers, Centre workers, they all seemed to be trying to stop him from being himself. They seemed to be trying to train him, as if he were a dog. So when he would do things like utter those statements from the movies I just mentioned, all of these so-called mentors and counsellors gave it a name, stimming, and then they tried to stop him from doing it. In essence, they were trying to stop his only method of communication. And it wasn't just the parroting, it was things like the goggle fingers and the way he would fidget with his fingers and twirl them around in front of his eyes. He also used to do the classic arm flapping when he was nervous, but he doesn't do that anymore. Anyway the experts, in the beginning, were all trying to stop these coping mechanisms. They were trying to stop him from communicating. They were trying to stop him from expressing himself. And it never did work and they never did learn. When all avenues ran out for my brother, when there were no coping mechanisms, and no way of getting his point across, he would go into a full blown panic attack. All that anxiety building up and exploding. And everything erratic and out of order and crazy. It was torture for Ben. He would begin screaming, screaming very loudly, because he didn't know what else to do. He would run to a corner and face the corner and put his hands over his ears. And they would come and gather around him and tell him his behaviour was unacceptable. And that was it in a nutshell, really. Ben's behaviour was considered abnormal. Their remit – and when I say 'they' I mean just about everyone assigned to him or anyone that cared for him – was to make by brother 'normal'. Make his behaviour acceptable. Because if Ben could be shaped into an acceptable contributing citizen, there would be nothing left for them to do. Their job would be done. Ben would be fine and, more importantly, society would be fine. And then society could wash its hands of him. (It's worth pointing out that it's different now. There is much better understanding of autism and the experts have a much better approach these days. Marsha is a good example. Ben loves Marsha.)

And anyway, it never works, does it? Trying to change people? And it's not as though Ben's anxiety will ever go away. It's always there. So, forcing him, wedging him, into society and doing things that go against his own instincts, this doesn't cure him, this just builds the anxiety inside him. I said before that all people with autism are different, and that's true, but there's one thing that I have found that they all have in common: they all need routine, and consistency – they need to know what to expect. And I say this, not as an attribute that is wholly 'autistic', I say it as an attribute that every single person on this planet has and needs. It's a human attribute. The breaking of expectation is simply more tolerable for most of us. For a person with autism, well, their reaction to surprise or unexpected change may seem out of proportion to most, but it's just a human reaction. My reaction is usually more stunted. I get the bout of anxiety in my stomach and feel like I'm going to be sick, and then I just move on.

Take a partner just up and leaving, for example. Am I supposed to pretend that it didn't make me feel bad when my girlfriends left me? I didn't scream and go and put my head in a corner, but I did go all foetal and cry for days and weeks and months on end. I know. I know it's not necessarily the same thing. And there are degrees of shock, tragedy and change in life. I am merely illustrating that it's not that much of a stretch to understand how someone like Ben might react when cornered with inevitable changes.

Ben's condition wasn't helped by my parents. My father stood as the aggressor, a person with little patience and a seemingly sadistic willingness to punish anything he believed to be out of line. He was a fucking monster. In many ways, he was directly responsible for setting Ben's development back many, many years. What a fuckwad! What a prick! *That scary man.* Unforgiveable!

And my mother wasn't much better, but to give her credit, she did turn it around somewhat in Ben's teens and in the years when I went missing (in alcohol and women). She stopped drinking and there was new literature coming through about autism and how to deal with it. In any case, all the years of pushing against Ben's instincts clearly hadn't worked. It was time to go with the flow and let Ben be the person he could be. So she stopped telling him to stop all of his parroting, echoing, and his funny gestures. She stopped being embarrassed in supermarkets. At some point, I think, she just stopped giving a shit about what people thought. Did she love Ben? I think she learned to love Ben in those later years. I think she did. I think when she stopped trying to fight him she began to understand what a sweetheart he really was. And that he was harmless. Sure, he was a little behind on some things, but truth be spoken, while he talks a little funny (in a kind of a robotic way) and while he may *sound* stupid at times, he was always pretty bright. And Mum began to see that. And then there were things he was super advanced at, like drawing and solving maths problems. She even displayed hints of pride at times.

The moment the world stopped pushing against Ben, Ben became what he always was, just another human. He became a human with odd behaviour, sure, but human nonetheless. And he began to learn and get enthusiastic about things. And his interests expanded and he began to enjoy talking to people, sporadically, more impulsively. Trust with strangers was still an issue, but what I noticed over the years, (and all the way up until now) was that Ben's trust was easier won over as the years went on. The other thing I would say about now is, if Ben doesn't trust someone, there is often a very good reason. Personally, I trust Ben's trust. If he reacts to someone as being an arsehole, he's almost always right.

When Mum was dying and Bridget was leaving me, it was obvious that Ben would move in with me. I remember Marsha having this conversation with me, down at the Centre:

'Are you sure you're ready for this?'

'He's my brother. What choice do I have?'

'He could be trained to live alone. We could put him through the self-dependency programme. It's not impossible, Howie. Of course you would need to supervise, but we could also get other supervisors to check in on him daily. It's been done before, and Ben, he's a bright boy. I think he is stable now, too, thanks largely to you.'

'I want to live with him.'

She looked at me a little suspiciously. Marsha is probably the smartest person I have ever met. She has a medical degree. She specializes in psychiatry in areas of intellectual disability and the like. She knows it all. But most of all, and this is what impresses me most about her, she understands me too. In fact, she can see right through me, right through the thin veils of my protective wall.

'Is this for you, Howie?'

'What do you mean?'

'You know what emotional dependency is, right? I see it all the time. I mean everywhere, outside the Centre. I see it all the time in what the world calls *ordinary* people. I had a friend who broke up with her husband and they shared custody of their three-year-old. She was emotionally dependent on that kid. She slept with the child for the next ten years and she was only ever okay if the child was around her. On those nights when the child was with her father, my friend was devastated. She used to call me up, sobbing, and I told her she needed to strengthen herself emotionally. She needed to see an independent *self*, outside of her relationship with her child. Do you see where I am going with this?'

'I think so.'

'I know you love your brother. I also admire the fact that, despite no training, you seem to understand autism better than many professionals I know. So you're qualified, that's for sure. But you should do it for the right reasons, Howie. And you should never forget yourself.'

I was getting a little annoyed with her. What was she saying?

Did she think my act was a selfish one? Or was she saying that it *should* be a selfish one?

'I think you're mistaken,' I said, 'if you think that I *need* Ben. There are two things to consider: One – Ben needs care and there is no one in this world better qualified than me to take care of him. And two – I *want* to live with Ben. I love him and he is fun. I really mean that. I enjoy being with him.'

'Good answer,' she said. 'I'm glad for both of you that there is a good solution.'

And now I have to confess that I am going somewhere with this. Without Ben I wouldn't have gotten to know the world of autism. I wouldn't have a job. But most of all, I wouldn't have this sense of empathy and love that I think he has helped develop in me. I wouldn't be me. You see, it's not just Ben I enjoy being with, I enjoy being with most people with autism. I find their integrity is strong and their sense of kindness is unmatched by so called 'normals'. And they are funny. Funny as hell. I don't mean funny to laugh at, I mean funny to be around and laugh with. I love their lack of cynicism. If something is beautiful, let's call it beautiful, people. People with autism, for the most part, in my opinion, are beautiful.

* * *

As said, I am going somewhere with this. This is the part of the story where I know, that anyone reading this, well, you would have every reason for fucking hating me for what I am about to tell you about what I did next. Like I've said before, I'm not proud of my actions. I can explain them, to an extent, but I am not proud of them. I can even justify them, at a stretch, but I am still unable to be proud of them. Oh fuck! I may as well just get on with it...

You see, I couldn't get Robyn's kiss out of my head. Robyn, that's right. Robyn, the woman that Ben met on *Love Is Mental.*

There was something special about that kiss. Have you ever heard a song called 'The Kiss' by Judee Sill? I listened to that song a lot around that time, and all I could think about was Robyn. (As a by-the-way, I often wonder why that Judee Sill song hasn't been used in a movie yet. Or has it? Anyway, mental note to self for future pub meeting: best song for a movie that's never been in a movie. Might require some research on my part.)

Of course I wasn't going to get in touch with Robyn. Her mother hated me and if the Centre got wind of me stalking her, well, there would be hell to pay. I would certainly lose my job and Marsha, what would Marsha say? Then of course there was Ben – what would Ben make of it all? No, that was out of the question. And yet, I couldn't stop thinking about her. I couldn't stop thinking about her kiss. And the more I contemplated that kiss, the more I felt the overriding anxiety (that had been plaguing me for months) start to dissipate. I really started to feel better.

I knew that I wanted another kiss like that. I thought about what to do for days and I came to only one conclusion. I realized that I should definitely date someone on the spectrum. And the more I thought about it, the more I made it make sense. Why not? Robyn's mother accused me of being exploitative, but she was wrong. I really liked Robyn and, as I've said all along, people are people, no matter if they have autism or not. There's no reason why someone like me shouldn't be attracted to someone on the spectrum, right? And at the end of the day, if I had a girlfriend with autism, who better would there be in this world to take care of her? I could love that person the way I love Ben. I could love both of them and take care of both of them. Why not? Didn't Marsha just say that I was better qualified than a lot of qualified professionals? Wasn't I the most qualified person in the world to be the boyfriend of a beautiful lady with autism? As far as I was concerned, this was a win-win scenario. But, and this was a big but, would the rest of the world understand?

Would society, who fights tooth and nail against anything it deems to be not normal, would society be accepting of such a thing? I had to think things through. And I thought and thought and thought and thought...

I concluded that the best way to go about this would be me faking autism myself. That's right. I would pretend to have autism and then surely all those doors would open and it would be easy to meet someone, without being judged, without being considered devious, and with everyone's support. I could go to an agency. I could find someone that shared my interests. I could find someone that would be able to kiss me like Robyn.

Judging me yet? Oh c'mon! It's not that much of a stretch, surely? (Justification City, here I come!) Think about it. Every day we leave our homes, we go out into the world and we put on faces. Someone asks us how we are and we reply 'fine' but inside we feel like shit and we are full up with anxiety and the dread of existence and inevitable death. Am I right? Okay, maybe not all of us feel that way. My point is that no matter who we are, we put on faces and we put on masks. We go to work and we are the colleague, the leader, the innovative new guy. We come home and we are the lover, the mother, the brother or the family man. We walk around with different masks for different occasions. We are the friend (even when we want to be more), we are the advisor, the sympathetic one, the customer in a shop. We're the indifferent commuter, the dog owner, the jogger, the rushed businessman. We're a million things. And we are all that and a million things more. And we all know this is true because our thoughts, no matter how together we think we are, are all over the place. We think things we feel we shouldn't. We imagine better lives. We fantasize that everyone in the world loves us, because we could be *special*. We dream of a better us. And millions of us's, scattered like stars in the universe, are bouncing around inside our consciousness at any given time. So is it surprising that we fall back to pretending? We don't know who we are. How could we? So we have to show something, pretend to be something, when we go out there, into the big world. We need an identity. We give ourselves a name, and we become that thing, that thing that the person we are talking to believes we are. And we deliver. We always deliver. Because that what's we call 'normal'. Whoa! This puts 'normal' into perspective, doesn't it?

So I ask, what could be wrong in me pretending to have autism? Really? Is it not just another mask? Okay. Okay. Okay. I know it's not, but you get the point – this is what I was thinking at the time. Fuck me… What a thing. To be me. To be *us*.

But my justifications went further than that. You see, as I've alluded to previously, I genuinely believe that autism, if accepted in one's environment, could be a beautiful thing. So I've said it before, people with autism, they have beautiful souls. Why wouldn't I want that for myself? Why wouldn't I want to be a beautiful soul? Couldn't I become a better person if I did this? And couldn't I help to make someone else's life better too? Again, I come back to the win-win. At the time I seemed to find justifications everywhere.

I am not so sure now. How could I be?

* * *

So the next step was to figure out how to fake autism. I sat down and tried to think of what it means to have autism. People talk about attributes and behaviour, but it's more complicated than that. As I've said repeatedly, they are human beings. And there is no one thing to cling to. They are as complex and multifaceted as anyone. It wasn't going to be easy. I started to think about Ben. Who was Ben? This narrowed the field down. I started to think about who Ben really was. And then it occurred to me that I was looking at everything backwards. Instead of trying to figure out who Ben was, wouldn't it be better to look at the things he wasn't? And that made so much sense, because I had so much more in common with him than otherwise. So why not focus on the different? I could make a list of attributes that the *ordinary* person has, that Ben doesn't have. It was brilliant. This was how I was going to approach it.

So I made a long list, and then I cut it down to a short list that would be easy to remember. And if I carried this short list around with me in my head, and kept checking myself, I might just be able to pull this off.

So here was the final shortlist. These are the things that Ben is not:

Dishonest
Cynical
Nasty or ill-willed
Greedy
Jealous or envious
Arrogant

I'm not saying there weren't other things on the long list that I could have added to the shortlist, but I had to keep it as short as possible. I had to keep it like a notepad in my head. And I'm not as smart as Ben when it comes to keeping notes in my head. That's the truth. He could be like an encyclopaedia at times. (An attribute that could not be faked and further confirmation that making a 'don't-do' list was better than making a 'do' list.)

So the goal was, if I could just cut out or close down as much as possible these instincts in myself, I could just about get away with it, I reckoned.

And here's the thing: who wouldn't want to cut out these attributes from their daily lives? These weren't admirable attributes. There was no positive side to these attributes. And when I looked at this list, I thought to myself, well, weren't these things the very things that I hated about myself? Who wouldn't want to fuck these things off? Couldn't this whole thing be an exercise in making me a better person? If I practised being this person, without these things, wouldn't I become a better person? Wouldn't that be so?

It makes sense, doesn't it?

It didn't take long for me to complete the justification circle. I knew I was onto something. I was convinced this was a good plan. I was definitely going to do it. Nothing was going to stop me now.

There were a whole lot of other, more practical things to think of. How would I go about finding a date, for example? I certainly couldn't go on national TV, on a show like *Love Is Mental*, for example. That would be suicide. There was also the problem with my association with the Mental Health Centre, who often worked with the dating agencies and, well, it wasn't the biggest of worlds – word gets around about these things. I also knew there would be an approval process. I would likely have to meet with the parents of my prospective new girlfriend, and I would, I suppose, have to convince them that I had autism.

I decided I would use Ben's identity. It seemed to tick all boxes and Ben wouldn't know, so it wouldn't harm him in any way. I looked a little like Ben. Not a lot, but the picture on his Disability ID Card was a bit fuzzy anyway. I reckoned I could get away with it (which I did, obviously). I would only go to one dating agency. A new one had opened in South London and it wasn't registered yet with the Mental Health Centre, so it seemed a good option, and one that wouldn't affect Ben if he later decided to go to other agencies.

So everything seemed to fit into place. The last thing to do was to take note of some small physical attributes and physical quirks of Ben's. They aren't so distinct really. His posture is a little stiff and he talks a little robotically. So I practised these things and worked on my 'don't-do' shortlist and I tried my best to emulate Ben's straightforwardness in conversation. I concentrated on the base-point of any kind of topic and looked at it in black and white. No grey areas. Everything to the point.

Say what came to mind. And most importantly, I could take my time. I didn't need to hurry conversation or pretend that conversation needed to go in a way 'normal' conversation would go. I honed in on a few topics and decided, as is often with people who have autism, to find two or three things that could be talked about incessantly. And that's where I had an advantage, I suppose. In truth, I could talk about anything. I could follow the woman's interests and fuel them. I could woo them, because I believed I knew how. Because I believed I knew better.

Now it was just down to finding the right woman.

Lastly, I got a crew cut, which surprised Ben. My hair had always been moderately long, but now I cut it and he told me I looked like him. I also wore my clothes in a different way. I started wearing Ben's clothes (collared check shirts, buttoned up), which he thought was odd at first, but then he delighted in it. And then I bought a pair of non-prescription glasses. The glasses were a fantastic touch. I looked at myself in the mirror and I talked robotically and I thought to myself: Yes! This is me! Why the fuck not? This is the true me!

* * *

One last note, before I move on to what happened next. I kept Ben out of this, of course. He didn't know what was going on. I sat down with him and told him I needed a little time to myself in the coming weeks. He was a little alarmed about changing the schedule, but he relented.

'I want you to be happy,' he said, and he set out with a long ream of blank paper so we could spend the next hour or so writing out a new schedule, in which I would get a weekday and some time on the weekend to myself.

It seemed easy to keep Chapstick out of it, as he was otherwise occupied at the time anyway. At that stage, we'd actually settled to just seeing each other at the football. (Despite Amelia doing a great job of turning my boy around, he was still an incurable gooner. And the new season was starting soon, and we were well excited.)

So, it wasn't that difficult to make all this happen. All I can say is that, by this stage, I was so well absorbed by the idea, that I completely forgot anything resembling common sense or ethics, or moral responsibility. I was on a mission and, with my crew cut and well rehearsed routines, I was too far gone to turn back. The long goal was to get a girlfriend, someone I knew I could be happy with, and to love and to be loved and to care and be cared for. Was it asking too much?

9

The agency was called *Love And You.* It was on the high street between a betting shop and an off-licence. Its logo was the initials and a heart with motion lines around it, as if it was beating. I didn't have the heart to be particular or say anything, but I am sure the agency workers were aware that the initials LAY were, perhaps, a little suggestive. But this was a minor detail. None of this really mattered to me, to be honest. I was excited and nervous, but also ready to get this assignment underway. It was time for me to be Ben and time for me to find love. To hell with the consequences. I was on a mission.

A nice lady called Charlize showed me to a chair in an empty room.

'Do you know how to use a computer, Ben?'

'Yes,' I said rigidly.

'Don't be nervous, Ben. We're your friends here.'

'Yes. Thank you.'

She placed a laptop in front of me.

'Here you have a questionnaire. We just want to know a bit about your interests and your hobbies. If you have any questions, Ben, don't be afraid to ask.'

The questionnaire was set out not only as a probe, to distinguish interests, but also as a base to distinguish possible roadblocks or potential problems. It was pertinent, I suppose, as any social interaction for people with autism is a platform for potential disaster. But as I was soon to find out, LAY had already done a bit of homework on me (or more pointedly, on Ben) by calling the Mental Health Centre. I made a mental note, as this could potentially cause problems, but I could already see ways around it. I could even delay Ben's next visit to the Centre, claiming an illness or something. In any case, perhaps no one would mention the fact that Ben was approaching a dating agency anyway. In any case, this was something that could be taken care of at a later date.

Charlize, who was wearing a long skirt and a flowery blouse, soon came back and sat opposite me.

'How did you find that?'

'It was easy,' I said.

'You know,' she said. 'You don't seem to be very much on the spectrum, do you?'

'They say mine is a mild autism.'

'Yes. That's good. And they confirmed that at the Mental Health Centre. They said you were very smart and very likeable.'

'That's nice.'

'So, we need to find someone for you, who's also likeable, and smart, and also has a mild form of autism. Do you agree?'

'That sounds ideal, Charlie.' I deliberately mispronounced her name and mentally congratulated myself on the move. I gave her a big grin.

She smiled back. She hesitated at the mispronunciation of her name. She thought of correcting me and then she thought better of it. I pretended not to notice. I thought about my 'don't do' checklist: don't be cynical, don't be nasty, don't be arrogant.

'So, Ben, you say here that your interests are football…'

'I like Arsenal.'

She nodded. 'Also, you like music.'

'Yes, but not all music.'

'Do you like rock music?'

'I like the Beatles.'

'Ah, very good.' She took down notes. 'You also wrote down space as an interest. How wonderful, Ben.'

'Yes.'

'Do you like watching movies about space?'

'Yes. The best ever space movies are: *2001 A Space Odyssey, Gravity, Interstellar* and *Alien.*'

'Isn't *Alien* scary?'

I smiled. 'Yes, a little.'

'Don't you like *Star Wars*?'

This made me hesitate. Oh shit. Wouldn't I like *Star Wars*? Yes of course. Ben loved the Star Wars franchise. I only pretended to like those films for his sake. Fuck! The list above was my list. Not his. I started to panic. My eyes started to shift. Fuck! How could I forget *Star Wars*?

'It's okay, Ben, you don't have to like *Star Wars*.'

'No, I do actually. My favourite all time character is Chewbacca.'

'Oh he is very nice, isn't he?'

'And tough.'

She took down notes.

Again I congratulated myself on my tiny little panic attack. It was confirmation of my (pretended) autism. Perfect really. And then it occurred to me: hesitating, forgetting and stumbling over things could only work in my favour. But I had to maintain that balance. If I could still worry, still feel anxiety over getting things wrong, the more genuine my little panic attacks would be. By the time I had thought all these things she had already asked me a new question, and I hadn't even heard it. (Another genius move!)

'I asked if you have a telescope?'

'My brother has a telescope.'

'And what do you look at?'

'It's hard to see things from London.'

'Of course.'

'But we look at the moon. And in the winter, when it's a bit darker, we can see four moons around Jupiter.'

'How wonderful.'

'Jupiter is my favourite planet. What's yours?'

'I think Saturn, with its rings.'

'The rings are ice.'

'Is that right?'

'Yes.'

'You *are* smart, Ben, aren't you?'

And this comment made me a little annoyed. Was she patronizing me? I wondered what her background was. Did she have experience with autism? I thought of asking her questions about her qualifications, but I realized that would be a little too 'normal'. I just let her carry on.

'So, Ben, are you going to be getting help with this? We usually have a parent come in with our clients.'

'My parents are dead.'

'Yes. I am sorry about that. But your brother, Howie, he takes care of you, doesn't he?'

'He says I am smart enough to do this by myself. He says that it's good for my independence and my self-esteem.'

'Well, good. You do understand that there will be a fee?'

Yes, and I also understood that the fee would be fully subsidized through the Centre. 'Yes,' I said. 'My brother, Howie, will take care of that.'

'Good. Well, this meeting was just to get to know you and get an idea of what you are looking for. What we are going to do now is use our database, and that's a database we share with the Mental Health Centre and also other agencies, and we are going to find you a partner.'

'What will she be like?'

'Well, I think, after meeting you, we have to find someone who is smart and who has a mild form of autism. And maybe someone who likes space. Someone who likes *Star Wars*, eh?' She winked at me.

'That would be wonderful.'

'We want to help you fall in love, Ben.'

'Thank you Charlie.'

Again she hesitated as if she was going to correct my pronunciation, but she again stopped herself. Instead she stood up and she shook my hand.

9

'Is it over now?' I asked.

'Yes,' she said. 'We have your number and we will call you soon. As soon as possible.'

It was only on my way home that I started to think about all the potential problems that could arise. How long could I get away with pretending to be Ben? And if I did find the love of my life with this, I would have to introduce her to the real Ben at some point. What then? I decided to take it as it comes. Would it be so hard to just tell the future girlfriend the truth? After I'd dated her a few times, and if it was working out, then I could just say something like, there'd been a mistake in the paperwork at the agency. That I really wasn't Ben, and that Ben was my brother. And then, I supposed, I could lead her to understand that in fact I didn't really have autism, but that I loved her anyway, and that everything would be okay and that we would all live together and we would be happy, etc.

In any case, it was happening now. I would just have to cross those roads when they came.

Well, I didn't have much time to think anyway, because the next day LAY got back and told me that they'd found a match. A woman called Rosalind. Would I be okay to meet her parents first?

'Yes,' I told them. 'I would be delighted to meet her parents.'

'And will your brother be available? They would really like to meet your brother too.'

This was going to be a hurdle. 'Yes,' I said. And then I thought that my 'brother', Howie, well, he was going to be sick when that meeting was to happen. It was all rather easy, really. Howie would have a really rotten cold.

So, to get my date, all I had to do was convince Rosalind's parents.

Oh fuck! Then I started to panic. And then I quickly realized that the panic was a good thing. I could use the panic. The panic would convince them. And then this thought calmed me down, which wasn't a good thing at all. I needed the panic back. And thus, my thoughts oscillated. But the more all these erratic thoughts buzzed about in my mind, the more I thought I could pull it off. Don't worry, I assured myself, on the day I will be full of worry.

* * *

The next day at work, Marsha, who stood at the front desk, looking calmly over her glasses at me, said, 'I hear Ben is going on a date?'

'Yes. What do you know about this new agency?'

'I've known Charlize for a while. She did some consultancy for us way back. She has a son with autism. She knows what she is doing. I think Ben is in good hands.'

'They've already found someone for him.'

'Yes, I know. Rosalind.'

'Is she with the Centre?'

'No. I mean, she's been around, but she's had great private care from the time she was a child. Her parents are very wealthy.'

'Oh?'

'She is your classic Asperger.'

'She is?'

'Yes. She has mild autism and savant syndrome.'

'She does?'

'She plays classical piano.'

'Oh.'

'I wouldn't have thought her a match for Ben, but I am trusting Charlize on this one. And, well, Ben is no savant, but he is very bright.'

'Maybe he will be a match after all?'

'One never knows, does one? I met my husband at the football.'

'You go to the football?' I couldn't hide my surprise. The last thing I would have penned Marsha to being was a football fan.

'No. Ugh! No, I went to White Hart Lane once because a friend of mind bought me a ticket. I didn't even know who Tottenham Hotspurs were. I thought their name was rather odd.'

I smiled. Arsenal's arch rivals, the team who shares North London with us. The team we like to beat more than any. The absolute enemy.

'Anyway,' she continued, 'I hated it all. I just don't get that game. I mean, men running about chasing a ball and kicking it. How is that fun?'

'Well, be thankful it wasn't golf.'

'What's the difference? You're still chasing a ball about, right? It seems like most sports are about chasing balls.'

'I suppose so.'

'Anyway, my future husband was sitting right beside me.'

'He's a Spurs fan?'

'He is.'

Oh Marsha. Oh, oh Marsha. Poor you, I was thinking to myself. I looked at her sympathetically and she laughed.

'My husband is a mechanic. He used to come home with grease under his fingernails.'

'A practical, worthy job.'

'We always have cars around us. He bought me an old Rolls Royce. It was impossible to drive.'

'Oh?'

'So you see where I am going with this, right?'

'I suppose so.'

'I've been with Trevor for thirty-two years, Howie.'

'Thirty-two years with a Spurs supporter.' This was unthinkable to me.

'That's right. And I still don't care one whit about the game. I don't care much for cars either. But I love Trevor. Trevor is a good man. The best of good men. Understand? He makes me laugh. I like the way he looks, the way he smells and what he wears. He cuddles me on Friday evenings and he pours my glass of wine and we watch Netflix and we still cuddle in our sleep.'

This was easily the most personal information I had ever got from Marsha, in ten years or so of knowing her. I had seen Trevor about, now and then, as he came to pick her up or drop something off. But of course, I would never be able to look at him the same way now, now that I knew he was a Spurs fan. Still it was gratifying to know that Marsha, at least, wasn't a Spurs fan. To be sure, she wasn't an Arsenal fan either, but at least she wasn't a Spurs fan.

'So,' I said, 'it's a lottery, isn't it?'

'Love is a lottery,' she agreed. And then she shrugged. 'Maybe Ben and Rosalind will hit it off? Keep me posted. I hope it all works out.'

And I couldn't help but think that the hole I was digging just got that little deeper at that moment (and it was going to get a lot deeper before the digging would finish). Now my boss, Marsha, was in on it all. She wanted to be kept posted. She wanted to hear how it turned out. She was engaged. She was paying attention. It wasn't supposed to be this way. It was all supposed to go under the radar.

Should I have pulled out at this stage? Should I have pulled the plug on the whole plan? The thing was, Rosalind sounded so interesting now. The agency had told me that she was interested in space, music and football. You heard it. I didn't know if she was an Arsenal fan or not, but I did understand that she lived rather close to the Emirates. It seemed only logical.

I had to meet her. I just had to. And what if it was just the one date, that would be okay, wouldn't it? In any case, I was determined. I wanted to find out who this Rosalind was.

* * *

Her parents invited me to lunch at an expensive restaurant in the middle of the city. A friend of theirs owned the restaurant, an amiable old fellow called Gino. Anyway, I had spent all morning working up my nervousness and awkwardness. By the time I got there I truly *was* nervous and there were tiny drops of sweat running down the side of my face.

'It's quite warm outside,' Angela, Rosalind's mother, said.

'It's been a hot summer,' Patrick, her father, agreed.

The meeting was set up without Rosalind being present. The parents were quick to assure me that they didn't want to intimidate me, or worry me in any way. They hoped I would understand that they just were looking out for their daughter, their very 'special' daughter. They just wanted to make sure that I would be gentle with her. They were hoping I didn't mind.

'I don't mind,' I said softly.

'I thought you were coming with your brother?' Angela said.

'He is sick,' I said.

I had been working hard on keeping my sentences short. *Just answer straight and honest, to the point, and no lies. Howie – no lies!* But of course, the first thing I did was lie, about my 'brother', Howie being sick. This apparent hypocrisy hit me as I sat down with them. It served me well. It made me sweat. It made my hands clammy and it made me overthink everything.

'Oh, I hope he's okay,' Patrick said.

'He has a cold. That's all. He said he was sorry he couldn't meet you.'

'And you came here on your own?' Angela said. Her eyes were big, forceful, but somehow gentle and understanding at the same time.

'Yes,' I replied.

'Bravo!' Patrick said, rather condescendingly I thought. But again, this thought wedged in where it never would with Ben. (Howie, keep it together, or, more appropriately, *don't* keep it together!)

'I try to be independent,' I said. 'My brother encourages me.'

'He sounds very nice.'

'Howie is the best.'

They told me to order whatever I wanted and I ordered some spaghetti, which I did my best to eat in an orderly fashion. I did manage to splash a little on the nice white tablecloth. Overall, however, they seemed impressed by me.

'You know,' said Angela, who I decided was kind and open-minded. 'You don't seem to be on the spectrum at all. You don't really show many traces of autism.'

Was this a good thing? Had I given myself away? What did I do wrong? I was doing the things I'd practised: fidgeting and talking with a mild robotic accent. I was giving short answers. I was avoiding the 'don't do' attributes (Well, excluding lying. It was only now, that I was in so deep, I realized that I wasn't going to be able to avoid lying. After all, everything about this plan was a lie.) Anyway, I thought I was doing everything right.

'Well, I mean...' she continued. 'We know you *are* on the spectrum. We talked with the Centre about you and they said you were the loveliest person. I must agree. You are a lovely boy.'

'Thank you. I think you two are nice too.'

It seemed I had passed the test. They asked me various questions about the things I liked and about how I lived my life: what kind of routines I had and what I liked most to do. And it seemed as if they were approving of everything. Truth be spoken, after a while I realized I had them wrapped around my little finger. By the time lunch was finishing up, I had to check myself constantly. I was a little too relaxed. I was a little too *Howie.*

I made a fuss about paying for my own lunch, which they found amusing and impressive. They didn't let me, of course, and I was glad about that, because I never have much money. And it was damn expensive. But they gladly paid and then they told me they would be happy for me to date Rosalind. They asked me if Saturday night would be okay and I said yes, though I wasn't sure what to do about the real Ben yet. In any case, I was now ready for my first date with Rosalind, and I couldn't wait. And at the same time I couldn't believe how smoothly everything was running. If I could convince her parents, I could convince anyone. I felt I was really going somewhere with this lark.

* * *

It all came down to a hot night in late August at the same restaurant I had met her parents. It turned out that, despite my protestations, there wouldn't be a bill to pay at the end of the night. Patrick told me on the phone that he was just chuffed that his daughter was going on a date. He told me to eat whatever I wanted and enjoy myself. 'Have a good time and don't do anything I wouldn't do,' he said cheerfully.

But, of course, this had me thinking. What would *he* do? And really, what were they expecting? And what was Rosalind expecting? For my part, I just wanted to get to know her and see what kind of a person she was. By the time the night came around, I had already convinced myself that it was unlikely I would be attracted to her anyway. So, in lowering my expectations, I felt that I could probably fulfil his wishes. (That I wouldn't do anything he wouldn't, if you know what I mean.)

There was a bottle of red wine on the table when I got there. It was to take the edge off, I suppose. I poured myself a glass, but also mentally checked: not too many tonight, Howie. Go easy on the vino tinto!

She came in and, I have to say, she was really good looking. She wore a summer dress that looked like something out of the fifties and she wore pale leather boots that had tassels streaming over her ankles. Her hair was black and her eyes were blue. They were big eyes, bright and alert. She flapped her arms a little when she saw me.

'Are you Ben?' she asked.

'Yes,' I said, remembering, above all, not to forget to act autistic.

'I like this restaurant,' she said as she sat down. 'My father's friend owns it.'

And then, on cue, Gino came up and asked us if everything was okay.

'Are you comfortable, Ros?' he said.

'Yes.'

'And you, Ben?'

'Yes, thanks.'

'Okay, well, enjoy the wine. It's an aged Barolo. A very good wine.'

And it was true. The wine tasted so good that I'd already drunk a whole glass in no time at all. I watched Gino as he looked at the bottle, noting I'd already downed a glass, and then I looked at the bottle myself and felt a little ashamed. But he just smiled at me.

'You two enjoy yourselves,' he said, and then he walked away.

'Would you like a glass of wine, Rosalind?' I asked.

She pushed her glass towards me and smiled. 'You can call me Ros, actually.'

It was hard to believe that she had autism. I mean, I am familiar with autism, but I found very few quirks in her. I immediately found her intelligent and interesting. She told me she was only allowed two glasses of wine. Or, at least, she only allowed herself two glasses of wine. I decided to make this limit for myself too.

'Me too,' I said. 'Otherwise I get a bit dizzy.'

She laughed. 'Drunk you mean?'

I liked her. I had convinced myself that it was too much to ask, that I would be attracted to her, but I really liked her right away. She had a nice smile and she used it a lot. It was obvious that she had a warm, joyful disposition. She also seemed to be quite comfortable, socially speaking.

'It's hard to believe you're on the spectrum,' I said.

'The same with you,' she said.

We ordered food and for the most part, Gino, who was taking care of us, basically recommended things and gave us suggestions, to which we seemed to say yes to everything.

'What colour is it?' Ros asked, when Gino recommended the Italian sausage risotto. 'I mean the palette of the whole dish?'

Gino smiled. It wasn't the first time he'd heard this question from Ros. 'It's red, darling,' he said. 'Just as you like it.'

Ros turned to look at me and smiled. 'I don't like anything green,' she said.

'Vegetables are green,' I said.

'Not turnips, or carrots, or beetroot or peppers or radishes or squash or cauliflower or eggplants or the inside of a cucumber.'

I nodded. 'Of course,' I said. 'That's a pretty good list.'

Everything about her was positive. She talked well. She ate well. She looked at me when I talked and she didn't show any hint of anxiety. And the conversation was lively and interesting.

'So you like football?' I was eager to hear if she was an Arsenal fan or not.

'No, not really.'

'Oh, they told me so at the agency.'

'They got that wrong.'

'What about space?'

'You mean, like, outer space? Oh, I love space. I like to watch programmes about space and I love the pictures. Have you seen the latest pictures from the Hubble telescope?'

I nodded enthusiastically.

'ESO 021-G004. 130 million light years away.'

I nodded. I had no idea what she was referring to. (Yes. Yes. I fucking know. I'm a liar. Liar. Liar. Liar!) 'What is your favourite TV show about space?' I asked.

'I'll give you a clue. *Billions and billions...*'

I started laughing and she started laughing too.

'Carl Sagan is my hero,' I said.

'Mine too,' she said. 'They told me you like music,' she continued excitedly.

'That's true,' I answered.

'The Beatles.'

'Yes.'

'I love the Beatles.'

She then took my hand and got me to get up and I smiled and I thought to myself, this woman's got spunk. Her enthusiasm was infectious. Anyway, there was this piano in another part of the restaurant. Rosalind asked Gino if she could play it and he said yes. And then Rosalind sat. She flapped her arms a little and she smiled at me, a big toothy grin. She then proceeded to do the most extraordinary playing of a piano I'd ever heard anywhere.

(A quick by-the-way, and mental-note-to-self to put it to Chapstick and Pontiac: greatest piano or keyboard players of all time – outside the classical music genre – in no particular order: Art Tatum, Ray Manzarek, Dr John, Bill Evans, Billy Preston, Tori Amos, Oscar Peterson and Professor Longhair.)

So, Rosalind went into this extraordinary musical montage that included a number of Beatles songs, some Bach, a bit of the blues and finished off with some mind-bogglingly fast jazz, or ragtime, or something. It was out of this world. She wasn't just talented, she was a fucking genius. Truly. And she did it all just smiling and occasionally looking over at me. It wasn't rehearsed. One could tell. She just played and segued into whatever came to mind. And all I could do was smile helplessly back. I loved it. This woman, well, what could I say? It occurred to me to use one of Ben's old catchphrases: *We're not worthy. We're not worthy.*

So, I asked her to play a few more tunes and there wasn't one single tune I put to her that she couldn't play. I tried to trick her, to make it more and more difficult, but she knew everything. I could hum to her a tune and she would quickly figure it out. I was completely blown away. How could she be this talented and not be the most famous person in the world?

She laughed when she finished and when she finally stood up, the people on the tables near the piano began to clap. She looked at me and said, 'You know, that wasn't me, it was the Asperger's.' She laughed and blushed, and then I saw, for the first time, a sign of anxiety in her face. Luckily Gino stepped in and ushered us back to our table, where the tiramisu (her favourite) was already waiting for us.

'That was awesome,' I said.

'I didn't really want the whole restaurant to listen though. And I got carried away, didn't I? A little too much, wasn't it?'

'No,' I said. 'You're brilliant, you!'

'It's not that great,' she said. 'I missed a few notes.'

'You should be playing professionally.'

'No way,' she said. 'I can't stand playing for people. But Mum and Dad, they said I should play for you. So I did.' She sighed and breathed out deeply. 'I was just so nervous doing that.'

'I couldn't tell,' I said, and that was true.

'Anyway, I don't really want to play for people. But I can play again for you.'

I couldn't help it, I suddenly felt intimidated. I mean, what was I compared to that? To that genius? I had no such talent. In fact, my brother (need I remind you, the *real* Ben) is far more talented than me. His drawing, though not considered a savant-degree talent, is extraordinary. And what about me? What were my talents? Pretty much fucking nothing. More like a talent for being a fucking liar and being, in general, someone completely and utterly unreliable. Fuck! It plagued me that she was so talented. It really got under my skin.

But she started laughing as she watched my face. She could clearly see that I was struggling with myself over who she was and, when it came down to it, who I was. She watched my contorted facial expressions and she let out a howl of a laugh. She could see all the compounded, unruly self-doubt. She smiled because she understood.

I was silent as I ate my dessert and finally she said, 'You really are on the spectrum. I can see that now.'

Thankfully, with my negativity threatening to brew and froth to the surface, the night was not lost and she told me she really enjoyed herself. 'I'd really like to see you again,' she said.

I thought about it, for just a few seconds too long.

'But it's okay if you don't want to,' she said.

But I did. I so did want to see her again. She was marvellous, in every way. Sweet, kind, direct, happy and so, so, *so* fucking talented. I really wanted to see her again. And then another part of me thought: leave her alone now, Howie. Leave this sweet lovely girl alone.

'I guess you don't really want to date again?' she said. 'It's okay, Ben.'

And then something else took over. Why shouldn't I? Why shouldn't I see her again? I made her happy tonight. And she made me happy. What on earth could be wrong with that? Why the negativity? Why be so down on myself? I could be this better person. I could be this person that could make this other person happy. I could make Rosalind happy. That was true. That was so fucking true and why the fuck shouldn't I?

'I really do want to see you again, Ros.'

She grinned. 'That's great!' she said.

And I smiled and she smiled and we hugged each other goodbye and we said things like: 'that was a great night' and 'it will be fun to do this again' and 'maybe we could go to the movies?'

The date had been successful. And there was more to come...

10

Their house in North London was old and big. It had a spacious garden out back and when one was sitting in the living room, one could look out through the floor-to-ceiling windows at the old white labrador lazing about on a big hedged-in lawn. It was my first time in her parents' house and I felt nervous. It was now two weeks since our first date and she was calling me her boyfriend.

We were sitting, facing the TV, and watching an old episode of *Friends*.

'I don't like sitcoms much,' she said.

'We can watch something else if you would like,' I said.

But neither of us changed the channel. We just watched. I laughed loudly at one of the jokes.

'Did you ever notice,' she said, 'that all sitcom humour is based on people acting autistic?'

I thought about this. A theory? I liked it. It actually made sense.

And then on the TV, as if to prove the point, Rachel and Monica got into a hysterical fight and started flapping their hands at each other.

'Tantrums,' I said.

'Exactly,' she answered, and gave me that you-get-it look.

'And Ross is always acting like a five-year-old. Come to think of it, they all act like toddlers.'

'Every single laugh is them acting like they are on the spectrum.'

'It's true.'

'And it's not just *Friends*. Think about it. *How I Met Your Mother. Scrubs. Brooklyn Nine-Nine. New Girl.* Oh, oh, oh, and don't get me started on *The Big Bang Theory*. They're all clinically diagnosable on that show, every single one of them.'

At about that time Angela came in and asked us if we wanted anything.

'Not me,' I said. 'I'm having a good time, Mrs Peterson.' And as the words came out I noticed right away that I had shifted my voice, made it more robotic and squeaky, just for Angela. And Rosalind noticed it too. She looked at me and smiled as if she was on to me, as if she knew it was all a lie, as if she understood everything.

'Well, just give me a shout,' Angela said. 'I'm in the next room.'

Maybe Rosalind did get everything. She was smart enough. But maybe at the same time she didn't care. Maybe she was just happy. We ask the least amount of questions when we are happiest, don't we? Those moments, when we seem to flow with the world rather than against it, don't we just go with it? Or at least we should. Isn't that where all the fun is at?

And the truth was, from both perspectives, everything was going swimmingly. It was so easy being with Rosalind. All of those fears about how I would pretend to have autism, and how I would implement this grand plan, and how I would fool everyone, well, all that slipped away when it was just me and her. With her I simply relaxed and became myself. And I think this made her more relaxed too, so she could be herself too. It didn't feel like there was any sense of autism, or obstruction, or hindrance of any sort toward us being together, or being happy together. We were going with the flow. And it was great. For a moment. It really was.

I don't want to pretend that there was nothing odd about Rosalind. She wore the same tasselled boots everywhere (boots I was beginning to dislike) and she tended to flap her arms a lot, especially when faced with new experiences. And her piano playing, as incredible as it was, it was odd – odd, to be sure, in a genius kind of way, but odd nonetheless. Sometimes I thought she was a robot. It was almost as if you could flick a switch and suddenly there was nothing she couldn't play. Well, I found out as time went on, she couldn't really improvise. I came to understand that. She could imitate improvisation, if that makes sense. She could listen to Bill Evans or Herbie Hancock and give it a little thought, and then she could imitate what they did. She could get the sound of it. She could follow the patterns and repeat licks. I suppose this could open a can of worms as to what musical improvisation really is – a vocabulary of learned licks, or a genuine impromptu language? (Definitely a conversation to be had at the pub.)

I should also point out, at this stage of my relationship with Rosalind, we hadn't kissed or done anything like that. And I mean anything. To this point there had been no mention of sex and, to be honest, I really hadn't thought of it. And I can't say that I needed or even wanted it. I was more interested in getting to know her, and getting to understand her, and learning to love and appreciate her for who she was. I wanted it all to mean something. Besides, I felt that she may be vulnerable when it comes to sex. What if she was a virgin? What if she was nervous about that? What if she didn't want that at all? It was my duty, I felt, to leave sex out of the equation, at least for the time being. Let her bring it up. Let it wait. It was something that should, I thought, arise organically. In any case, to this point, it had not been brought up. And if there was a kiss to be had, well, it would come. I was quite content to wait.

We dated most of September and, as the autumn came on, things just seemed to get better and better between us. I had to fit her into my regular life somehow, and that wasn't so easy. Ben was becoming a bit befuddled as to how many times he had to change the refrigerator schedule that month. But he was tolerant, and he kept telling me that it was okay if I wanted to do my own thing. He said that he was okay to take care of himself. I couldn't introduce him to Rosalind yet, because I had the not so uncomplicated task of having to explain, not least to

Ben, but also to Rosalind, why my real name was not Ben, but Howie, and why it was actually my brother who was called Ben (and who was the one with autism). I didn't have a plan yet as to how to overcome this, so I decided, for the time being, to take things day by day, and let things happen as they come. (So, as you can see, faking autism was, in essence, really impossible. All the contradictions. All the hypocrisy. The idea of a person with autism taking things day by day, and letting things happen as they come, well, that's just ludicrous. Nothing would terrify Ben more.)

Anyway, for the moment, I kept Rosalind away from my regular life. I didn't even tell her about Ben, or Chapstick, or anyone. How could I? It would make me too normal. I couldn't take her to the football (although she wouldn't have wanted to go anyway – too loud and not nearly interesting enough), which was a damn pity, because the Arsenal were shredding at that time. No, I just had to keep her out of those things, for the time being, until I came up with an ingenious plan to integrate it all – my normal life with my extraordinary life with Rosalind. It would work out, I assured myself. I was so sure, cocky even. But boy was I wrong.

However, I can't deny it, I had a wonderful time that September with Rosalind. We did so many things together. We went to all kinds of restaurants, but especially Gino's, as it was always for free. We went to museums and art galleries. We had record nights. (Just for the record, she was mostly into classical music and so these nights were somewhat educational for me – Bach, Chopin, Shostakovich – but not as fun as record nights with Chapstick. She didn't like jazz much, although I opened her up a bit to some piano greats and she recognized patterns and commented on them from a technical point of view.) She couldn't go to concerts, unfortunately, as she found them too loud and disturbing to enjoy. She did take me to the opera to see *Madame Butterfly* and I actually thought it was very cool. We also did silly things like going to London tourist spots. We even went on the London Eye, and she really liked that. She seemed to have no fear of heights whatsoever.

'Why do they call it an eye?' she asked me, as we started going upwards.

It was one of what I had come to think of as her 'trick questions'. Trick questions were: her asking me a question with a logical answer, but if I were to answer logically, well, I would be giving myself away as 'normal'. Sometimes I just wanted to think like her. I mean, sure, it's obvious to most why it's called the London Eye, right? You 'see' a view of London from it. But this answer was a little too easy. Hence the trickiness of it all. (This situation arose all the time with Rosalind. I had to be constantly on the ball.)

'Yeah,' I finally said. 'It's not like it looks like an eye, or anything.'

'Wouldn't it be funny if eyes were really round, like people say, instead of oval-shaped, like they are?'

'That would be very freaky.'

'I wonder what aliens look like.'

'Me too.'

This was a pretty typical conversation. I tried to mostly let her lead conversation. I had always found that this was best for Ben too. Or at least, it was the least stressful thing for Ben. If he, or Rosalind, could control conversation, they could control the flow of all social intercourse. It was quite straightforward really. And it worked. It was completely okay with me. I had no need to control conversation at all. And anyway, and I kid you not, she was so much more interesting than me. And my voice, that voice inside my head that was always talking, well, shit, I already had to put up with that 24/7. So, having her lead in conversation, it was refreshing and interesting.

A standout incident came up in the last week of September. We went to the Science Museum, and we were standing in line for the IMAX cinema. We had chosen to go and see a documentary about the solar system. She had never been to the IMAX cinema before, so I was very excited for her.

Rosalind was looking at the posters on the wall, posters of well-known movies.

'*Avatar* was nice but silly,' she said.

'Yes, I agree,' I said.

'Could there possibly be anything more silly than the word *unobtainium*?'

I couldn't stop laughing. It was something that I had always thought but had never said to anyone. And then a question occurred to me: was Rosalind cynical? Was I wrong about autism and cynicism being opposites? Could those with autism learn cynicism? And was she, actually, being cynical? Maybe cynicism is a function of intelligence? Maybe it's hardwired? I was absorbed by these thoughts when she said:

'You like *Star Wars*, don't you?'

'No,' I said.

'Yes you do.'

'No,' I repeated.

'It was in your file.'

'No it wasn't.'

Okay. I could go on like this. Because this discussion didn't end there. Oh no. I wish it had ended there.

'You told them you like *Star Wars*.'

'No, I didn't.'

Yes, I did. I remember it now. But at the time, outside the IMAX cinema, I couldn't remember that. I insisted she was wrong. This was our first disagreement and, before I knew it, her eyes were starting to shift about madly and her hands began to tremble.

How could I be so stupid? Why did I need to insist I didn't like *Star Wars*? I mean, who cares, right? Why couldn't I just let her be right? She *was* right. But when I said, 'you're wrong' so definitively, well, that completely freaked her out.

She screamed at me and hit me and as I tried to calm her down she threw my arms away and she stormed off. Everyone turned around and looked at me. I could even see a few people shaking their heads. I assumed that they assumed I had done something bad to her.

Perhaps I had.

Fuck! And I looked at my watch and the movie was going to start in five minutes. Fuck! Fuck! Fuck!

I got out of line and went searching for her. I started to panic after a while because she was nowhere to be seen. Eventually, after a half hour or so, I found her in the geological section of the museum. She was looking at stones.

'Hey,' I said.

'I like moonstones,' she said. 'It's like a mother of pearl, or a cheap bargain-bin opal.'

'I like them too,' I said. 'Are you okay?'

'*Sodium, potassium, aluminium silicate.* Moonstones.'

'Do you want to go and see the movie now?' I said, again looking at my watch.

'Has it already started?'

I nodded.

'No. It's too late if it's already started. I don't like missing the beginnings of movies. Let's go home, Ben.' She took my hand and she smiled at me. 'I want to eat pizza.'

* * *

At the pub on a Saturday night. We'd just beaten Everton at home and Chapstick, Ben and I were in a pretty buoyant mood. In fact, we hadn't really seen each other in some weeks, so there was a general feel-good atmosphere about us. At that time, Chapstick and I weren't doing our record hunts anymore, and record-listening night, well, that had also become non-existent.

He explained that his relationship with Amelia was going really well, and he wanted to give it every chance. 'I don't want to blow it,' he said. 'I always blow it.'

'I know what you mean.'

I fixed Ben up on a stool and pretty soon we got served three plates of pies and fries. Ben was a little disappointed, however, as he wanted mash. 'And gravy,' he said nervously.

It was Andy that was serving. 'Oh shit,' he said. 'Sorry Ben. It's the new waiter. She got it wrong. I'll take it back.'

'No, it's okay, Andy.'

But Ben wrapped his Arsenal scarf tighter around his neck and he ate his meal in silence and was a little grumpy.

Later, when Ben strolled over to the TV to watch a replay of the big game that day – between the Citizens and the Scousers – I decided to run Rosalind by Chapstick:

'I'm seeing someone,' I said, a smile on my face.

'Really?'

'You sound surprised.'

'I thought you said you were done with women.'

'And you said we are never done with women.'

We both chuckled and shook our heads. *Us… eh?*

'What's her name?' he asked.

'Rosalind. She's a musician.'

'Professional?'

'Nah. She is too shy. But man, you wouldn't believe it. Talk about Bill Evans, Elton John, Mozart, you name it!'

'Mozart?'

'She prefers classical music.'

He nodded. 'So when do we get to meet her?'

'Soon,' I said, hesitant. 'Soon.'

'You know, I never did ask you, but what happened with you and Rita?'

'The meter maid?'

'Yeah.'

'I guess the chemistry wasn't right.' I looked at him and I was slightly suspicious. 'So Amelia didn't say anything?'

'No. What about? You and Rita?'

'Yeah.'

'No. Rita said you were nice, that's all.'

Rita said I was nice? That was a turn up. *Really*? I looked over at the match and they were replaying a disallowed goal and I could see a few fans in the pub pointing at the screen and shaking their heads. Rita? *Really*? She thought I was nice… I really didn't see that coming. I mean, I couldn't even get it up. How could she like a man who couldn't even get it up? I suddenly felt even smaller than usual, if that were even possible. Like a little schoolboy. Sure, she thought I was nice. Sure thing! *She* was nice. That was the truth. *She* was fucking nice. We're all nice. Yes. I got it. She was just *being* nice.

'Anyway,' I mumbled. 'Rosalind is great.'

'I look forward to meeting her.'

Pontiac came in, got himself a beer and joined us at the table.

'Gents.'

'Pontiac.'

'I suppose you've heard the new Dylan record?'

That was certainly enough to shift my thoughts.

From Rosalind to the great Bob Dylan.

'It always amazes me,' said Chapstick, 'when I hear that people like his early stuff, but not his later stuff. I mean, are they even listening?'

'He's been pretty much on-song since *Time Out of Mind*,' I said.

'Well, you know me. I like the earlier stuff,' Pontiac said, as if being deliberately contrary. 'But I have to say *Rough and Rowdy Ways* is a really good record.'

We all agreed.

'I've been thinking,' said Chapstick. 'I've had plenty of time to think about this one, as you know, when you start seeing someone, music gets second place for a bit.'

'No,' said Pontiac. 'Not with me. Music first. Always. If a woman comes into my life, she better damn well be into music.'

'When was the last time you had a girlfriend, Pontiac?' I asked.

'Been about five years now,' he said.

I nodded. It made sense. It made perfect sense. I was so glad at that second that I had Rosalind. I didn't want to be like Pontiac. I didn't want to put music first. I wanted to put love first. What's wrong with love? And then it occurred to me: I *loved* Rosalind. This put a massive smile on my face.

'Anyway,' said Chapstick. 'We always talk about the greatest this and that. And you know, we always come to the same conclusions.'

'Not always,' said Pontiac.

'Well, it's Beatles or Stones. Or Beatles or Dylan.'

'It's never Beatles or Stones,' I said. 'I don't think you can put the Stones in the same category of greatness as the Beatles. Maybe the Stones and The Who?'

'I'd choose The Who,' said Pontiac quickly.

'I don't know,' said Chapstick. 'But that's not what I wanted to say. I mean, what does *great* mean anyway? I figured you could split it into two categories: influential and genius.'

'That's interesting,' I said. 'Go on.'

Pontiac nodded.

'Dylan's legacy, surely, is his influence,' said Chapstick.

'There isn't one musician in the field of pop or rock that comes after 1965 that isn't influenced by Bob Dylan,' I said.

'Not sure about that,' said Pontiac.

'Yes, that's what I mean,' said Chapstick. 'What is there after "Like a Rolling Stone"? In my opinion it's the first song in history that sounds like everything we listen to now.'

'I think I see where you are going with this,' I said. 'It's a mistake to compare the Beatles and Dylan. Even the Beatles were influenced by Dylan.'

'"You've Got to Hide Your Love Away",' said Pontiac.

We nodded.

'But the Beatles,' Chapstick said, 'were pretty much inimitable.'

'What about bands like Oasis?' queried Pontiac.

'Oasis sound like a tiny piece of the Beatles jigsaw,' said Chapstick.

'Right,' I said. 'Like John Lennon circa 64 or 65.'

'As a whole,' said Chapstick, 'the Beatles were just too musical. Those melodies. Not many people can write like that and, even if they can, they don't have the sheer variety and range.'

Both Chapstick and I looked at each other and were both nodding and mentally patting each other on the back. 'Good theory,' I said.

Pontiac put his fingers on his chin. He was thinking of a comeback. He wasn't so convinced.

All this conversation did was highlight how much I missed Chapstick. And I think he missed me too. We just looked at each other and smiled.

'Great game today,' he said.

I nodded. I wished that I could tell him I missed him. I wished that I could just say: 'Hey, we should hang out more'. I mean, couldn't we have girlfriends and still be best mates? I chuckled to myself. We needed to draw up a schedule, I thought to myself. We needed to make time.

* * *

September came and it went, didn't it? Doesn't it always? And the more I got to know Rosalind, the more I liked her. We laughed a lot. That seems to be a common thing to say when people are talking about how good their relationship is. *We laugh a lot.* But all relationships have to get serious at some point, don't they? And I ask sincerely, don't they? With *utter* sincerity. I mean, *do* they? What is it about relationships that ultimately lead to a seriousness, to a sense of dread, to an ultimatum or a blank? They have to go somewhere, don't they? They have to travel. And if you travel far enough, you know it's going to go deep. And isn't that the meaning of depth? Seriousness, that's what lies in the deep. The serious and fucking scary.

Now, as it came up not long ago, I refer to the fine art of sitcom making again. Now, I am not going to disparage them, the way Rosalind dismissed them. They have their purpose. And they're funny. Am I right? Well, not always. You see the longer a sitcom goes on, the further they travel, the more deep they have to go. Where else can the writers go? Sure they can keep turning out well-worn gags (although these too have their limits) and the characters are going to keep behaving like children, but at some point, those characters, in one way or another, are going to have to grow up. And let me tell you, growing up isn't that funny. Actually, it's hardly funny at all. Because you grow up and then you get even older than that. Until you're just fucking old and of course you still laugh now and then, you know a good joke or two, and you can behave like a kid sometimes, because, just now and then, it's endearing, even charming, but one day you're going to have go deep. You're going to have to try and get a grip. Because the closer you get to death (fuck me, what a thing!) the more fucking serious you're going to get. Don't fight it. The writers of sitcoms can't fight it. At some point a heart will break, at some point a child will be born, at some point a character will get married and fuck knows, they are going to have to grow up then, because someone out there will be crying. That's right. They'll be sitting in front of their TVs and they will cry because such and such was about to get married, but such and such says the wrong name or sleeps with the wrong person or leaves the other such and such at the altar. And it's a breakup. And it's sad. And people cry and you can't deny that. And then it's not comedy anymore. Then it's life. And, as a writer, you've got nowhere to go, nowhere to hide, nowhere your bum doesn't stick out. Because the irrefutable fact is that life is finite. Everyone dies. And, well, there's nothing funny about dying at all.

Rant over. But you'll see where I'm going with this momentarily.

Rosalind asked me, as we were sitting at Gino's restaurant, eating our third free tiramisu each, the most important question concerning our romance:

'When are we going to have sex?' she asked. She was smiling. She knew it was a prickly topic, but it was time, she thought. And, all said, she was rather relaxed and matter-of-fact about it.

'I don't know,' I said. I suddenly became nervous, which was just as well, because she understood how difficult this whole matter was, when it came to those on the spectrum.

'Are you a virgin?' she asked.

'No,' I said. And then I broke the 'don't do' rule again. I lied: 'I did it once, with a girl from the Centre.'

'Oh.' She looked slightly disappointed.

'What about you?' I asked innocently.

'No. I've never had sex before. I'd really like to.'

'I know,' I said. 'Me too. But we haven't even kissed yet.'

And then she leant over the table and gave me what was possibly the worst kiss I have ever had. It was all teeth, and clumsy, and slobber, and just, well, horrible.

'I've never kissed anyone before,' she said.

I tried to smile. 'You have now,' I said.

'Okay, so we've kissed now.'

I nodded.

'So we should do sex. Even my parents say so.'

'They do?'

'Yes.'

'Okay. But maybe next week, okay?'

'Yeah, that's okay. I am free on Wednesday afternoon.'

'Me too,' I said.

'Let's do sex on Wednesday afternoon.'

'Okay,' I said.

On the way back to the apartment that night I started to panic. How did I get myself into this? It was all a lie, of course. I realized that now. It was all wrong. I couldn't explain why. I just knew it. I couldn't have sex with Rosalind. No. Of course I couldn't.

But didn't I like Rosalind? Didn't I just say I *loved* Rosalind? Yes. Yes! What the fuck was wrong with me then? I decided I had to go along with it. I just had to. Even her fucking parents wanted me to fuck her. For goodness' sake! I could do it, I thought to myself. And I would teach her. That was it! Yes! I would teach her how to have sex and I would teach her how to kiss properly. Wouldn't that be a good thing to do? Wouldn't that even be the right thing to do? Wouldn't that be helping her?

But did I want to? I thought about it. I wasn't sure. And then there was my last venture into sex, with Rita, which of course had been an utter failure. What if that happened again? How on earth would Rosalind handle that? And what did she know about sex anyway? Presumably, if her parents were so keen for her to get off with me, surely they had taught her a thing or two? Holy shit! What was I saying? What was I thinking?

And then Wednesday came all too quickly and I thought I was ready but I was as nervous as fuck. We were at her parents' place, as they'd gone off to France for the week. So we were on our own. I sat down in front of the TV and nervously drank a glass of water. The labrador ambled over to me and fell asleep on my feet.

'Do you want to do sex first?' she asked. 'Then we could watch some TV later. We could watch a movie.'

'Is there anything good?'

'Yes. There's some good movies just released by Netflix. *The Joker,* for example.'

We looked at each other. I put my hands in my pockets.

'Okay, so let's do it,' she added, a little too angsty.

'Do you think we can postpone it, Ros? I've got a bit of a headache.'

'Oh, okay. Let's watch *The Joker* then.'

She sat down beside me.

And then something happened that set things off. The TV wouldn't turn on. It had, apparently, inexplicably, stopped working. I looked over it and checked all the connections, but I couldn't figure out why it wasn't working. I'm not the most technical of people, but I thought I could work it out. But I couldn't. And all the while, Rosalind sat on the sofa, nervously watching me fuss around the TV. She was becoming more and more anxious. I told her not to worry but I could see tension building up inside her. I suggested we do something else: play a game or something, or do a puzzle. But then, suddenly, out of nowhere, she burst into tears. And then it got worse. She started screaming at the TV. She hurled the remote control at the TV and it dented the screen. I looked at her bewildered, unable to comprehend why she was overreacting in this way. And the more bewildered I looked, the crazier she became. She completely flipped out and ordered me to leave immediately.

'But…' I mumbled.

'Fuck off!' she screamed and threw a book at me.

Right. So… One might think that that would be the end of things, right? So surely I would pull the plug on this thing right there, right then, right? Well, let me tell you a little more about myself. I am far more stubborn than that. I am far more resilient. Far more stupid, too. And anyway, I'd been around people with autism, or more specifically Ben, all my life. She was upset, for sure. Unduly upset. And out-of-proportion upset, for sure. But was I to give up on her, just like that? Would that be right or fair?

She called me up hours later and she told me she was sorry. And then she said, 'I really like you, Ben.'

'I really like you too, Ros.'

'I am in love with you, Ben.'

And I heard myself saying the following: 'I love you too, Ros.'

It just slipped out. It was almost as if this ball had been set to roll and this was the particular hill it was rolling down. I couldn't get out of this now, could I? And this was the thing, it wasn't just a sense of guilt or a sense of duty driving me, I really did care about this woman. Like I've said, she was the sweetest, loveliest human being. She was dead loveable. Sure she threw a tantrum, but that was just her way of expressing herself when all other measures had been exhausted. You see, I *did* understand. She wanted to have sex. She had got herself ready to have sex. And I rejected her. Who wouldn't be upset with that? She had every right. She had every right to be angry with me. And wouldn't I rather be with someone who showed their anger rather than hold it in? (Last train to Justification City! All aboard!) I owed her my affection. I owed it to her, and I owed it to myself. Everything I had set up here, *everything*, it was okay. It would be okay. We would work this out, together. I couldn't, wouldn't, give up on her this easily.

I asked her to meet me at a café in town the following day, and we could talk. I told her everything would be okay.

'I love you,' she said.

'I love you,' I said.

Argh!

* * *

End days are nigh. Bear with me. The story takes a nice little twist right around now.

10

Rosalind and I sat at an outdoor café, on the edge of a park in North London. (Not far from the Emirates, it turns out.) We were talking about everything that had happened the previous day and she said she was just nervous, that was all.

'I don't know why,' she said and her face drooped a little.

'I know why,' I replied.

'Why?' she asked.

'Because it's not easy, that's why. Whatever anyone tells you about relationships, they're not easy.'

'Yes. And I feel like I just have to have sex, you know? Because they do it in the movies. And everyone does it, really.'

'If you believe what you read, everyone seems to be doing it all the time. Everywhere.'

'Exactly. But Ben, we don't have to do it if you don't want.'

'We will,' I said, and I meant this. I had come around to the idea that it was right – right for her and right for both of us actually. 'We will do it soon.'

'Okay, Ben.'

And then, as if walking from a blurry mirage, coming down the street, walking like she'd always walked, her lips smiling and ready to laugh, was Bridget. She looked assured, happy in an alone-happy kind of way. She looked like she'd lost weight since I'd last seen her. And her face looked tanned, as if she'd just returned from a trip to southern Europe. I really couldn't believe what I was seeing. My heart raced. This was the woman I had loved above all others. This was the woman that I had thought about, lying in bed alone, unable to sleep, for over a year after our breakup. This was the woman whose leaving hurt me more than all the others put together. Bridget. And she was walking towards me.

I instantly panicked, of course, but there was no time to escape. She had spotted me and she was headed my way. Her smile began to bare teeth. Her beautiful teeth. Her dimples. And the Howie-is-that-you look on her face.

'Howie?' she said.

Rosalind looked at me with curiosity. *Howie?* What was going on?

'Hi, Bridget. How are you?' I said. 'What are you doing in London?'

She took a double take on me, as if she was trying to figure out if indeed I was Howie. 'Howie, you sound weird. Why are you talking that way?'

'What do you mean?' I said.

'You're talking weird. Like a robot.'

'This is the way I talk.'

'Why is she calling you Howie, Ben?' asked Rosalind.

I ignored Rosalind and looked directly at Bridget. 'What are you doing in London?'

'I've moved back. I was going to call you...'

Bridget smiled at Rosalind and she held out her hand, which Rosalind promptly ignored. 'I like your boots,' Bridget said to Rosalind.

I could see Rosalind was starting to wring her hands. Her face was blushing. Her eyes were fidgeting from side to side. She was going to go into full-blown panic mode, any second now.

'What's going on, Howie?' Bridget asked me.

'Why is she calling you Howie, Ben?' asked Rosalind again, now agitating in her seat. 'Isn't Howie your brother?'

'It's complicated, Ros. A case of mistaken identity.'

Bridget just looked at me and squinted her eyes. She gave me a look I had seen many times. A look that said *who are you*? But she quickly decided that this wasn't her problem and that she had already heard enough. 'Well, I don't know what game you're playing here, Howie, but I'm out of here. Sheesh. I thought you'd be happy to see me.'

'I am.'

'Bye bye, Howie.'

Bridget walked away and I wanted to call after her but I was lost for words. And then there was Rosalind, just fuming, sitting in her chair, about to lose the plot.

'Don't worry, Ros. I just look like Howie. It's happened before.'

'Who is she?' she asked as she calmed down a little.

'She's...' but I stopped talking. I looked at Bridget's back. I watched my ex walk down the street. I watched the woman that I had loved more than anyone, ever, walk away from me, again. She had moved back to London! For all I knew she could still be single. And here I was, playing games with a poor, lovely, beautiful woman with autism. What a fucking douche bag! What a fucking animal! What a fucking lying, cheating, stupid-ass, unworthy fuckwad.

'She's...'

She's just the love of my life, I wanted to say. *She's just about the only person I ever really loved.* Fuck! Fuck! Fuck!

I looked at Rosalind and I knew there was only one way out of this. I said to her, slowly, but surely (with not a trace of a robot in my voice), 'C'mon Ros, there's someone I want you to meet.'

She looked at me, saw the sincerity on my face, and she took my hand.

We took the tube across the city and I took her, for the first time, to my apartment. Ben was there, doing a puzzle. He looked at Rosalind and me as we came in and he declared, 'I cleaned the place, Howie. It's really clean.'

'It's perfect, Ben. Just perfect.'

'Ben?' Rosalind said, slowly, as the penny began to drop. 'So you're Ben?' she said to Ben.

'Yes,' said Ben.

And then she turned to me and said, 'And you're Howie?'

'Yes,' I said.

You would think that this surprise would send her reeling,

send her into a fit, but she simply stood there and looked at Ben, and then looked at me, and then back at Ben again. She didn't say anything for a while. And I have to give her credit. She remained calm, even in the face of this unexpected shift. And it made me think. It made me realize she was so much more than I had ever given her credit for. And it made me come to the conclusion that she had somehow figured me out, long ago. That she knew that I'd been lying all along. And that somehow, she knew that it would all end up this way, and that it would all be okay.

She smiled. 'Okay,' she said.

'Do you want to do a puzzle?' Ben asked her.

She looked at him and shrugged. 'How many pieces?' she asked.

11

And, well, that almost brings me up to date. All that stuff went down just last week and, fortunately for me, there were very few recriminations or consequences for my wayward actions. Rosalind's parents never called me up so I really don't know what they made of the whole fiasco. And Rosalind and I have remained in touch. She really likes coming over and hanging out with both Ben and me. She never said that I hurt her. She just said that I had disappointed her. But in the end, she said: 'It's okay, Ben, I mean Howie. Oh, I am going to have to get used to that.'

But there is still a bit of this story left – a bit of the story involving Bridget. In the last few days I have met her twice. So, let me tell you about that.

I won't lie. After the impromptu meeting in the park café, I thought of nothing else for days but calling Bridget. I felt I owed her some explanation. It was such a weird meeting. I wanted to explain. But then I thought: what the hell am I going to explain? Was I going to tell her the truth? She would think I was dirt. She would think I was the lousy scum that she probably always, secretly, knew I was. And that was where the problem was. What the hell could I say to her? And anyway, what did I want? What did I *really* want?

I kicked myself. What if she was single? What if she would have given me another shot? Did I just fuck that up? Forever?

Anyway, as you can imagine, I didn't call. I just got on with life. I decided that it all went down the way it went down and that was the way it was meant to be. Rosalind wasn't for me, clearly, and neither was Bridget. Who the fuck was I kidding? There wasn't a fish out there for me. No way, no how. It would be Ben and me. And that would be it, for the rest of our lives. It made me cry to think this. And I couldn't tell you if those tears were for a loss or a gain. I could do something so mundane as watch my brother doing a puzzle for hours and tears would well in my eyes, I loved him so much. All this should be enough. Am I right? It was meant to be just Ben and me. Maybe *Ben* was the love of my life?

We went to the game on Saturday. The season's first North London Derby. Chapstick, Ben and I were really pumped up. We got off the tube and marched to the Emirates like foot soldiers.

'We better win today,' I said. 'I really need a win.'

'We will,' said Chapstick. 'Don't worry. We've the better team.'

'We're going to win,' said Ben. 'Don't worry, Howie.'

We got to our seats and there, in the row ahead, was Bridget. She'd decided to join her aunty (Badger), who managed to get her the seat beside hers.

'Hey, stranger,' she said to me.

'Hey,' I said. 'About the other day.'

'Yeah what was that? Very weird.'

'Ah, that was a friend of... Ben's.'

'Oh, I figured.'

Over the loudspeakers, the teams were announced. We watched as the players came running out onto the pitch.

'C'mon Gunners!' yelled Mickie Jones.

Bridget smiled and started cheering.

'This is where we met,' I said.

'Yeah,' she said. Then she greeted Ben and I could see Ben's eyes light up.

'You look beautiful,' he said to her.

'I agree,' I said. 'You lost weight.'

'You always said you liked me as... What was the word? *Voluptuous*?'

I wanted to tell her, right then, that I liked her in all ways, and it didn't really matter how she looked at all. I liked *her*. But I kept my mouth shut and grinned and shrugged.

The game started and pretty soon Mickie Jones was swearing and cursing, particularly at the referee. I put Ben's earmuffs on him.

When Spurs scored, Badger turned around to Ben. 'Never mind, love, there's still plenty of time.'

'We're going to win today,' said Ben confidently.

And we did win. We scored twice in the second half and we all jumped about, particularly because the second goal came in the eighty-ninth minute. Spurs looked dejected and we all took glee in watching them, heads bowed, leave the pitch.

I even got to hug Bridget. She was wearing a different perfume, I noticed. But I couldn't put my finger on what it was. It was a grown-up scent, like citrus, like a lemony herb garden. And before we disbanded I asked her if she would have lunch with me.

'Are you asking me out?' she said.

'It's lunch,' I said.

'Ah, so not a date.'

'I just think it's so nice to see you, that's all. It would be lovely to catch up properly, don't you think?'

'How very adult of you.'

'Well, don't get ahead of yourself. I'm still me.'

'Sure, let's have lunch,' she said and she shook my hand, as if completing a business transaction.

* * *

I met Bridget today for lunch. And now, as I sit on my bed listening to a very distinct snore coming from my brother's bedroom, I am unsure of how I feel. Life just dishes up uncertainty, doesn't it? It offers very little in the way of the concrete. It makes me think of the Van Morrison song 'Enlightenment'. I mean, what the fuck is anything? What is the truth of anything? Is there any truth out there? And that's where I come back to my brother's autism, and how he copes and how he sees the world. The very essence of grey, of the un-understandable, is his nightmare. Van the Man's song is an utter terror for Ben. (Mental note: don't ever play it to him!) It's almost as if Ben, the truer human, the more *human* human, is the purest result of the billions of years of evolution. I'm the illusion – the misfit. He's the reality, because, at the end of the day, what isn't scary about the unknowable? We *should* be scared. We should all be scared. I've developed into someone that pursues distraction and I call it an interest. But my interests aren't interests, really, they're coping mechanisms. It's nothing short of survival we're talking about. But Ben, Ben sees the world as it really is: grey, fuzzy edges – inexplicable. He sees it as too big, too wondrous, too awesome. And then, oh boy, if you think about the whole universe, well, you're well and truly fucked. And that's where my thoughts are going, from Bridget to the universe. It seems a logical segue of thinking. I mean, it's all a mind-fuck, isn't it? Think about the sheer size of it all, and that, in truth, we don't really know the true size or the true age of the universe. We know as far as we can see. And we can't see very far. And that's the sum of it really. What are we supposed to assume beyond what we see? It's ambiguous, to say the least. Ben understands this. Rosalind understands this. Robyn, and all those kids down at the Centre, they understand this. We can trust what we see. Everything else is overwhelming.

I said to Marsha, just yesterday, as I was leaving work: 'I wonder what it is,' I said, 'to look through their eyes.'

She grinned and looked at me with a you-don't-get-it look.

'What?' I said.

'Why don't you try looking through your own eyes?'

'Not sure what you mean, Marsha.'

'Love,' she said. 'You think it's ambiguous. It's not to them. Love is concrete to them. You give them love. They give it back. That's what they see through their eyes: love. A world with it, or a world without it.'

Oh, yes. Fuck it! She was right, of course. Why is love so grey to me? Why is it so grey, messy, so indefinable and so impossible? Why can't I see it?

Bridget sat at a small table inside the big window of a chain café. It was raining outside and I had come out in shorts, a tee shirt and a baseball cap.

'I thought the summer was never going to end,' I said, as if by way of excuse.

'You're an idiot,' she said, almost laughing.

'That's true.'

We hugged and this time it wasn't because the Arsenal had just scored. This time it was because once upon a time we used to sleep together and feel each other's feet under the blankets.

'It's good to see you,' she said quietly.

We ordered coffee, she with an extra shot, and we looked outside at the rain and the blustering umbrellas.

'So what happened with the south coast? Too hippy for you?' I asked.

'I loved it. But Mum got sick recently. I needed to come home and take care of her.'

'I'm sorry to hear that.'

'Well, it's not over for her. She had a stroke. She just finds it a little too hard to do the daily stuff. You know what it's like. With Ben and all.'

'Ben's become quite self-sufficient.'

'I always admired your patience with him. You know, you can be a good man sometimes, Howie.'

I turned away. I drank from my coffee and made a silly remark about someone struggling through the rain, ill-dressed.

Bridget shook her head.

'Will you go back down south?' I asked.

'Maybe. But for the moment I am actually quite happy to be back in London.'

I thought about my next question before asking. Did I really want to know? I hesitated, and then I smiled, and then she smiled back at me.

'So, no boyfriend then?'

'I had one for a couple of years down there. But he left me for someone else.'

'Oh no.'

'It's okay. I think it turned out that they were better suited for each other. They're actually close friends of mine now. They're having a baby.'

I looked at my coffee solemnly. I suddenly became nervous. I let her talk and she talked about the lifestyle down there, how she got a job in a pharmacy, how she loved the band scene and she'd also begun playing guitar.

'Oh really. Are you any good?'

'I've played a few gigs. Joni Mitchell songs mostly. Open tunings. I love Joni.'

'Me too. One of the greatest female songwriters of all time.'

'Ah, correction: one of the greatest *songwriters* of all time.'

I laughed and nodded. 'Of course. Maybe the best of all time.'

'You'll have to run that by Chapstick,' she said winking.

I breathed deeply. Here it came:

'Bridge, why did you leave?'

Well that took the conversation away from Joni, but somehow, segueing from Joni to our breakup, it didn't seem that much of a stretch to me. (Just listen to *Blue* if you don't know what I mean.)

She just looked at me and shook her head. 'Does it really matter?' she asked.

'I just feel like I never understood.'

'You never do, Howie. You think the world is understandable, or worse, controllable.'

And there it was, the grey funk, like a cloud, descending upon me again. I felt like I was in a smoke filled room, cancer-giving smoke, and looking for a saviour that would show me the door. Where was that guardian angel? Where was that guiding light? Where was that God? I understood everything about religion in that second. Everything.

'No,' I said pathetically.

'You're cynical. You're a liar, or more specifically a self-deceiver. You can be mean. You can be greedy. When we were together you often got jealous. You envied everyone. *Everyone*!'

So, everything on the 'don't-do' list. Fuck me!

'You pretend,' she continued. 'Always pretending to be something else, or someone else.'

'Like pretending to be Ben, for instance?'

'You don't get it, do you?'

'What do you mean?'

'You *are* like Ben. In every single way. And that's both good and bad.'

'There's nothing bad about Ben.'

'Stop idealizing him. You're the one that always says he's just like everyone else. You make him out to be an angel. He's human, Howie. That means both good and bad.'

'Not sure I get what you mean. I really fail to see the bad.'

'People with autism, just like anyone, can be self-centred and self-absorbed. Ben can be that and you know it. And I know dominating conversation is a coping mechanism, a way of controlling, but it's not a good human trait, is it?'

I looked into my coffee. A feeling of guilt mixed with overt anxiety overcame me. I wanted to escape, escape to a corner and look into it and hope to find comfort there. I wanted to look at a night sky or listen to Pink Floyd. I wanted to scream too. And I started thinking about football. Our next game. Who was the manager going to play in central defence?

All of this amounted to me being the monkey with its hands over its ears.

'Most of all...' She wasn't finished yet. 'When we were

together, you were self-obsessed. It was all about *your* interests. You talked about your football, your music, and your space...'

(My space?)

'And you didn't leave much room for anyone or anything else. You never seemed interested in me.'

'Sure I was.'

'What were *my* interests, Howie?'

'Umm... You liked movies. Socializing.'

'Everyone likes movies and socializing.'

'You liked design.'

She looked at me curiously. She liked *design*? Oh dear, I was thinking of Carrie.

'You didn't know me, Howie.'

'Yes I did.'

'And therefore, it stands to reason, you couldn't have loved me, Howie.'

'But I did. Bridget. I loved you the most.'

'The most of what?'

'Of any of my girlfriends.'

She laughed.

'I do love you.'

'Oh leave it out, Howie.'

We looked at each other a long while. She went to drink from her cup and then her hand stopped, mid way to her mouth.

'Like I said, you can be a good man, Howie. Look at what you do for Ben. If only that side of you, that unselfish side, could be channelled into other parts of your life.'

'I guess I am selfish, really. Look at the mess I create around myself.'

'Don't start wallowing. *That's* autistic. *That's* controlling. If you realized how good you are, or could be, you might be able to love someone, you know?'

'I love you.'

'No, you don't!'

And she got up and started arranging her things. 'I've got to head,' she said.

'Why don't you wait till the rain stops?' I said, imploring her.

She gave me a knowing smile. 'The rain never stops, Howie.' And then she started to walk out of the café.

'Bridget,' I said abruptly, and she turned to look at me.

'Yes, Howie?'

'What about catching up again?'

'I don't think so, Howie.'

And then she left.

Well, I wasn't going to go back out into the rain. I was still wet from when I arrived. So I went and ordered another coffee and it struck me, just as I was paying the woman behind the counter, that the rain *was* never going to stop. I handed over the cash and I walked out of the café, without the coffee.

Part Three

12

Today was a good day. Today my best friend got married. That's right. Eddie Song (aka Chapstick) tied the knot with his beloved Amelia. And I want to talk a little about the wedding. Because it was nice, and lovely, and I was the best man, of course, and because everyone I cared about was there. But first, let me catch everything up.

It's March – six months or so since I met Bridget at that café. Six whole and long months. But the last six months have been blissfully grey. Nothing to see here. Or nothing much. At the very least, I don't feel guilty or embarrassed about anything I have done in the last six months. Sumptuously non-eventful, I would say. Or at least in the sense of 'me'. Things have happened. Things always happen. Good things too. It's only – they've happened to others.

Ben and Rosalind have a solid thing going on. That's an event, I suppose. They came out of his room one day and they told me, matter-of-factly, that they just had sex.

'Oh,' I said.

'What's on TV?' asked Rosalind.

But they must have liked it, because they did it again, and now, each time they do it, they report it to me. And I can tell you, it's often. Once they got a taste for it, they didn't know when to stop. I did ask them, at one stage, if they couldn't do it a little more quietly.

'Why, Howie?' asked Ben.

'You sound like when you go to the toilet,' said Rosalind, and they both laughed.

'Charming,' I said. 'Well just keep it down. You might wake the neighbours.'

'The neighbours are doing it too,' said Ben.

'Everyone's doing it,' said Rosalind. 'Everywhere. All over

London.'

And that was the end of that. I couldn't fight their logic. There were two of them around me now. So much logic and common sense. So much black and white. So much scheduling.

'I love you, Howie,' said Ben.

'I love you too, Ben.'

'I love you too, Howie,' said Rosalind.

'I love you too, Ros.'

Truth be told, I couldn't possibly be happier having those two around. And I couldn't possibly be happier for Ben. They have found love. And I am going to do all in my power to help them both to make it work.

Marsha told me to stay out of it. She told me I'd mess everything up. But I asked her: 'What could be more scary than love?'

'That's your problem,' she said. 'Not theirs.'

So fair enough. But fuck that sideways anyway. Sure, I am not intervening or anything. I am not telling them how to fuck (or 'make love' as Ben corrected me one night) or how to be in love. I am just there, for when the microwave doesn't work, or when it's hard for one of them to explain themselves. It's love. Am I right? Let's not idealize this. One still needs to express oneself and be understood. It's not that easy. Give me a break.

Anyway, I've never seen Ben so happy. And Rosalind, well, Rosalind is happier, much happier than I could have ever made her.

And just as a side note, Rosalind's parents were okay when I told them the truth about everything. Well, let's say it was close to the truth. I told them that I was merely checking out Rosalind for the real Ben. It was all part of some elaborate plan. They thought I acted weirdly, to be sure, but as they got to know me over the succeeding months, they laughed it all off. They could see Rosalind was happy. And they thought Ben was nothing like me. And, well, Bridget was both right and wrong about Ben and me being alike. I can see that now. But still, Ben doesn't do things on the 'don't-do' list. He doesn't even know what those things are. Those words, like liar, cynic or arrogant, they aren't even a part of his vocabulary. That list simply doesn't even exist for him. It doesn't need to.

Bridget and I have become friends. After that café meeting I did some thinking and I realized that I had wasted so much time, and I was wasting so much time. What could be clearer than someone saying no to you? Does it matter why she left? (Well, apparently yes, because clearly I had a fucking lot of lessons to learn.) The point is, she doesn't love me, and she never will again. It was just to let it go. And the day I did let it go, I called her up and asked if she wanted to go and see a new band I liked. She was unsure and then I said: 'You know, I like you Bridget. I want you to be in my life and I don't love you anymore. Okay?'

She laughed and since then we've been hanging out quite a bit. She's even started seeing this guy she met at one of the gigs we went to. He's a Palace fan, but that's okay. I always liked the Palace fans. (As long as they are lower down the table than us, all good.)

And that brings me to my beloved Arsenal. No, we're not going to win the league (probably never again, by the looks of things) but I have to say, we sure know how to lose in style. We are challenging, at least, for a Champions League place, but I don't know... Our arch rivals have been fucking steaming this year, and, well, they might just pip us again, as they have for many years now. That's life. I actually met a Spurs supporter, a woman, in a pub and we went home and had sex and we had a really nice time together. But it wasn't to be more than that. (And that had nothing to do with football.) Her name is Naomi and she's also a friend of mine now. She's a trooper and she doesn't take the football that seriously. And, well, maybe I don't anymore either. Ah, well, maybe I do. Whatever... We go on, don't we?

* * *

And now the wedding today. What a day! It was a beautiful sunny Saturday afternoon. Luckily Arsenal were playing away, up north, but we weren't focusing on that, naturally. (Okay, they lost, but who cares? Am I right? *Much.*) We converged on a tiny brick chapel in our local area. I was a little nervous as I stood with Chapstick at the altar. Across the way I could see Rita, who kept making childish faces at me, which made me laugh. And then the bride entered. She looked astonishing and I watched Chapstick's face light up and I just wanted to be him. I badly wanted to be him. But I kept all that in. This day was not going to be about me. I convinced myself that I'd left my selfish me at home, and now, it was all about Chapstick. Of course it was about Chapstick.

And then the song rang out. 'You Take My Breath Away', sung by Eva Cassidy. Now, don't get this mixed up with 'Take My Breath Away', that shit-synth-pop-80s-crap by Berlin. It wasn't that. It was much better than that. And it worked. It really worked beautifully, as she glided down the aisle.

But, well, now I can't help myself. Let me rewind a little, to a Saturday at the pub, just a few months before, when Chapstick brought up the idea of the aisle-walking song with Pontiac and me.

'It's got to be emotional,' I said to Chapstick.

'It has to be something Amelia will like,' said Chapstick. 'Only, I've been wracking my brain and I'm struggling. I really am. I need your help, guys.'

We all looked at each other, realizing the gravity of this moment. Chapstick was asking us to choose the most important song for the wedding.

'Right. This calls for another round,' said Pontiac. 'Same, fellas?'

We nodded and he went off to the bar. When he came back,

beers in hand, he said: '"I Can't Help Falling in Love With You".'

'I don't think Amelia would like that much. But Elvis, man, what a crowd pleaser.'

'Yes. Good choice,' I added. 'Did you think about "Amelia"?'

'The song? She loves that song,' said Chapstick. 'But it's about Amelia Earhart. If only we could change the lyrics.' He looked at us long and hard. 'She really loves Billie Eilish.'

'What's there not to like?' I said.

'Not for me,' said Pontiac.

'"Ocean Eyes"?'

'That's going on the shortlist,' Chapstick said, scribbling it in a notebook. 'But I have to check the lyrics.'

'What about a tune without words? "It Never Entered My Mind"?'

'Nah,' said Pontiac. 'You have to have words.'

Chapstick agreed with Pontiac.

'There's always Chet. I've never met a woman who doesn't like Chet.'

'I've got it!' said Pontiac. '"Tennessee Whisky"?'

'Yes!' I declared, and the three of us broke into the chorus of 'Tennessee Whisky', ending on those immortal lines about staying stoned on love. We laughed when we finished.

'Stoned on your love might be a little controversial.'

'"She Belongs to Me",' I said.

'I thought about that,' Chapstick said. 'I thought about it long and hard. I really wanted to somehow shoehorn a Dylan song in. But there's something in Dylan's voice at that time. A sneer. If you know what I mean?'

'Yeah,' I said. '65 was a sneer year for Dylan.'

'"You Take My Breath Away" – the Eva Cassidy version!' said Pontiac.

We all three looked at each other and nodded. Here was a song that was instantly likeable yet not that well known. Bingo! Pontiac knew he'd found it. He stood tall. He was so proud of himself.

'That will tick all boxes,' said Chapstick. 'All age groups. The whole demographic. And the lyrics are a perfect fit.'

'Who doesn't like Eva Cassidy?' I asked.

'There's the further advantage,' said Pontiac, 'of her being dead.'

Oh yes, the good old 'die young theory'. We didn't need to run through that one again. It was a conversation from many years ago. The overrated-because-they're-dead theory. A good one but, alas, that was for another day.

When Amelia walked down the aisle, I saw a tear in Chapstick's eyes and then I quickly found one in my own. This was disrupted, however, when Rita began poking her tongue out at me. I began to laugh and it was almost as if the whole procession stopped and everyone, particularly Chapstick's parents (who never really liked me) glared at me. I coughed, as if to make out that my laugh was really a cough. Rita looked at me and shrugged, taking no responsibility for her part in the disruption. And then, with the words of the over-reaching celebrant, Chapstick and Amelia were joined in matrimony.

* * *

There's only one brief thing left to comment on. Later, as the party settled into dancing (I couldn't get Ben and Rosalind off the dance floor) and drinking and general shenanigans, I walked outside and lay on some grass and looked up at the night sky. I felt good, about myself and about life. I wanted to share that with space. Because, well, space needs my smallness, doesn't it? I mean, what would space be if it wasn't for me lying there, thinking about it and defining it?

Out came Rita, carrying a bottle of red wine and two glasses. She lay down next to me. 'Hey,' I said. 'You can just about see Jupiter if you look real hard.'

'Or if you *hardly look*. You really are a nerd, aren't you?'

We smiled at each other and she bent upwards and poured a glass of wine for herself, and then one for me.

'So I hear you guys talk about nerdy music theories all the time,' she said, as she lay down again.

'Sure,' I said.

'I have one.'

'Go on.'

'If you take every love song, and replace the word *me*, with *meat*, it makes the song better.'

'It does?'

'Every time you go away, you take a piece of meat with you.'

I laughed, so much so that my glass began to wobble and I spilled wine on my white shirt. I looked at her and I thought she was just about the most beautiful thing I had ever seen.

'Hello,' I sang. 'Is it meat you're looking for?'

A message from C.C. Howard

Thank you for reading *So Very Mental.* I sincerely hope you enjoyed it. I would be so grateful if you could take a few moments to add a short review on Amazon, Goodreads or Apple iTunes Store. Reviews mean everything to authors. Each and every one of them is hugely appreciated and can, in so many ways, encourage new and better stories in the future. To keep abreast of my new and upcoming novels and short stories, visit my website www.cchowardauthor.com or follow me on twitter @CCHowardAuthor

FICTION

Put simply, we publish great stories. Whether it's literary or popular, a gentle tale or a pulsating thriller, the connecting theme in all Roundfire fiction titles is that once you pick them up you won't want to put them down.

If you have enjoyed this book, why not tell other readers by posting a review on your preferred book site.

Recent bestsellers from Roundfire are:

The Bookseller's Sonnets

Andi Rosenthal

The Bookseller's Sonnets intertwines three love stories with a tale of religious identity and mystery spanning five hundred years and three countries.

Paperback: 978-1-84694-342-3 ebook: 978-184694-626-4

Birds of the Nile

An Egyptian Adventure

N.E. David

Ex-diplomat Michael Blake wanted a quiet birding trip up the Nile – he wasn't expecting a revolution.

Paperback: 978-1-78279-158-4 ebook: 978-1-78279-157-7

Blood Profit$

The Lithium Conspiracy

J. Victor Tomaszek, James N. Patrick, Sr.

The blood of the many for the profits of the few… *Blood Profit$* will take you into the cigar-smoke-filled room where American policy and laws are really made.

Paperback: 978-1-78279-483-7 ebook: 978-1-78279-277-2

The Burden

A Family Saga

N.E. David

Frank will do anything to keep his mother and father apart. But he's carrying baggage – and it might just weigh him down ...

Paperback: 978-1-78279-936-8 ebook: 978-1-78279-937-5

The Cause

Roderick Vincent

The second American Revolution will be a fire lit from an internal spark.

Paperback: 978-1-78279-763-0 ebook: 978-1-78279-762-3

Don't Drink and Fly

The Story of Bernice O'Hanlon: Part One

Cathie Devitt

Bernice is a witch living in Glasgow. She loses her way in her life and wanders off the beaten track looking for the garden of enlightenment.

Paperback: 978-1-78279-016-7 ebook: 978-1-78279-015-0

Gag

Melissa Unger

One rainy afternoon in a Brooklyn diner, Peter Howland punctures an egg with his fork. Repulsed, Peter pushes the plate away and never eats again.

Paperback: 978-1-78279-564-3 ebook: 978-1-78279-563-6

The Master Yeshua

The Undiscovered Gospel of Joseph

Joyce Luck

Jesus is not who you think he is. The year is 75 CE. Joseph ben Jude is frail and ailing, but he has a prophecy to fulfil …

Paperback: 978-1-78279-974-0 ebook: 978-1-78279-975-7

On the Far Side, There's a Boy

Paula Coston

Martine Haslett, a thirty-something 1980s woman, plays hard on the fringes of the London drag club scene until one night which prompts her to sign up to a charity. She writes to a young Sri Lankan boy, with consequences far and long.

Paperback: 978-1-78279-574-2 ebook: 978-1-78279-573-5

Tuareg

Alberto Vazquez-Figueroa

With over 5 million copies sold worldwide, *Tuareg* is a classic adventure story from best-selling author Alberto Vazquez-Figueroa, about honour, revenge and a clash of cultures.

Paperback: 978-1-84694-192-4

Readers of ebooks can buy or view any of these bestsellers by clicking on the live link in the title. Most titles are published in paperback and as an ebook. Paperbacks are available in traditional bookshops. Both print and ebook formats are available online.

Find more titles and sign up to our readers' newsletter at http://www.johnhuntpublishing.com/fiction

Follow us on Facebook at https://www.facebook.com/JHPfiction and Twitter at https://twitter.com/JHPFiction